EDWIN SPENCER
MISSION IMPROBABLE

J. D. IRWIN

Catnip

The format details for this book are;
Arial, Bold 24, Single Spacing

FOR ALEX

CATNIP BOOKS

Published by Catnip Publishing Ltd 14 Greville Street
London EC1N 8SB

This edition first published 2010
1 3 5 7 9 10 8 6 4 2
Text copyright © J. D. Irwin, 2010

The moral right of the author has been asserted.
Cover illustration by Andy Parker
Cover design by Mandy Norman

A CIP catalogue record for this book is available from the
British Library.
ISBN 978-1-84647-095-0

www.catnippublishing.co.uk

National Blind Children's Society has been helping visually impaired children and their families since 1995.

The Charity is unique in its focus on young people who face different challenges as they grow up. National Blind Children's Society is special in that it offers solutions, tailored to individual needs.

Technological developments create possible new learning experiences for the visually impaired, but too often these life-changing aids are beyond the financial reach of many families. National Blind Children's Society provides a vital service, ensuring through the supply of specially adapted computers, large print books, advocacy and grants that children receive the help they really need.

If you would like to help National Blind Children's Society in any way at all, please contact our offices on 01278 764764. We look forward to your call.

Contents

CHAPTER EIGHT

THE NEXT MORNING, EDWIN AND PERPEFUA were up before the birds. They'd barely slept, and decided to get some fresh air at the top of the castle. Lorius hadn't been mentioned yet – they were both waiting for the other to break the silence.

'What we saw last night could mean anything,' Edwin blurted suddenly.

'That's what worries me,' Perpetua grumbled. 'Doesn't it worry you?'

'A bit ...'

Perpetua tut-tutted. 'Lorius took the dagger that killed Auvlin and hid it ... mad old ladies are one thing, but that's different.'

Edwin let his gaze wander, picking out bales of hay in distant fields. 'Let's think about this. Janus told us that Lorius took care of Auvlin's body when it was brought to the castle ... he didn't say he'd ordered the dagger to be destroyed. Maybe ... maybe Lorius thought it ought to be kept as some sort of relic, but thought Janus wouldn't approve.'

'So why did you sleep on my floor last night?' Perpetua snapped.

'It was seeing the dagger ... you know, the murder weapon.'

Perpetua didn't say anything. She just stared straight ahead.

'Listen,' Edwin added. 'I know Lorius looks like something off a Wanted list, but he's served Hysteria for thirty years. What could we do, anyway? Tell Janus that Lorius has got the dagger – wouldn't we get in trouble for spying on him?'

Perpetua crossed her arms. 'It depends on what we found out.'

'But it could be totally innocent. And if Lorius was up to something, why would he have tried so hard to get me here ... to help Janus? If he's some sort of traitor, that doesn't make sense.'

Perpetua raised her eyebrows. 'Yes ... but there's something here that isn't right.'

'But it's none of our business. We should keep our noses out and get on with what they've asked us to do. Lorius hasn't hurt us, has he?'

Perpetua shook her head.

'If he was going to, I think he'd have done it by now. Janus trusts Lorius – who are we to question that?' Edwin stepped down from the battlements and held out his hand. 'Come on – let's see if Ollwin's ready. His lessons are the best, aren't they?'

Perpetua stared at Edwin for a moment, then gave a grudging nod. She looked a little brighter as they made their way down from the terrace, and Edwin felt the heavy ache in his stomach start to slip away.

The next few weeks sped by faster than an ice-cream van in January. Lessons with Ollwin almost doubled; Primus took Edwin and Perpetua horse-riding every morning, and within a few days they could both steer and trot. Evenings were spent helping Bellwin practise apprentice tasks, so they had little time to think about Lorius or Mersium, or any other mysteries that had troubled them before. Even the sight of Auvlin, lying in the depths of the castle, seemed like a distant memory.

Ollwin reminded Edwin and Perpetua again and again that their introduction into the Hysterian Court drew near. At the end of a particularly long afternoon, he smiled and stepped off his lectern.

'Rejoice, my friends! You have learnt all you need to take part in a full state banquet. And with good timing – your first is tomorrow night!'

'You mean we've finished lessons?' Edwin said hopefully.

'Yes. And I think you have earned yourself a splendid lunch!'

Edwin and Perpetua were ushered away, but she suddenly turned on him. 'Are you stupid? We've done our basic training and tomorrow night we're going into battle. Honestly, Edwin, no wonder you can't pass a test. You can't even spot when one is coming up!'

'Get lost! I'm just glad we've got a break.'

'A break? There's no time for a break – we should start revising right now!'

'No!' Edwin said finally. 'I'm not going to muddle my brain any more. We promised Bellwin we'd give him more time – that's what we should do.'

For once, Edwin got his way and they met Bellwin that night. He'd worked all day on the crystals, and was exhausted by the time he came to Perpetua's room.

'Look what we saved for you, Bellwin!' Perpetua cried as he slumped onto her bed. 'Junoberry cordial. Janus sent us some for lunch and after I drank it I was full of energy.'

'Yeah,' Edwin sighed. 'Imagine the most annoying person you know, then triple them.'

'Right, we've got the orb thing covered,' Perpetua said, ignoring him. 'So what's the next task you'll be tested on?'

Edwin guffawed. 'Is it, how to spot a know-all?'

Perpetua blinked. 'Well, Bellwin – what is it?'

'It is a difficult spell,' he answered. 'I have to tune a person's mind into a sound or a voice – one they would otherwise not be able to hear.'

'Something far away?'

'Yes. If done properly the spell would be able to catch a sound – or someone speaking – on the other side of the castle. Will you be the subject, Perpetua?'

She shot to her feet. 'I'd love to!'

'This may not work the first time,' Bellwin said cautiously. 'But I will try for any sound or any voice.' He raised his left hand and whispered, 'Vocalia tunetarium.'

Perpetua stood still and screwed up her eyes. After a minute, she opened one lid. 'I can't hear a thing.' Bellwin shook his head. 'You may be trying to hear the voices They should come to you.'

'Sorry ..'

'Calm yourself,' Bellwin instructed. 'Let me try again. Vocalia tunetarium!'

Edwin could hear Perpetua's steady breathing. Suddenly, her head jerked.

'I can hear something!'

'Be quiet!' Bellwin snapped.

Perpetua did as she was told. She frowned, scowled, pulled an exasperated face, then looked around the room, blinking.

'What did you hear?' Bellwin and Edwin chorused.

'It was a woman she seemed to be talking in her sleep or something. She said "Our work here is almost done" and "It grows steadily".'

'That sounds a bit mysterious,' Edwin said.

'There are countless servants in this castle,' Bellwin replied. 'And they are all kept very busy!' He clapped his hands. 'It must have been dear for you to hear all that, Perpetua! Edwin, do you want to try?'

'No thanks, I've seen more magic than you can shake a wand at.'

'As you wish.' Bellwin squeezed Edwin and Perpetua into a bear hug. 'I am more ready for Ollwin's tests than ever – and it is thanks to you, dear friends!'

Edwin laughed and pulled himself free. 'Can I get to bed? I've had enough of studying to last me a lifetime!'

The next evening, Edwin was in his room waiting to be taken down to the banquet. He was dressed in a gold crown, a heavy tunic and a long fur-trimmed robe. He could barely stand let alone walk, but was trying to move like Auvlin. Head up, long strides Ollwin had said. Edwin sidled in front of the mirror and attempted to look imperious, but decided he resembled Perpetua on one of her don't-even-speak-to-me-'cos-I'm-dead-brainy days.

Edwin delved into the back of his wardrobe, grabbed a biro from his blazer pocket and made a few notes on the back of his hand. He'd just finished when there was a knock on the door and Janus appeared.

'May I come in?'

'Yes, Your Majesty. Have you come for me? I was expecting a servant ...'

'I want to talk to you on the way to the Great Hall,' Janus replied. He studied the room. 'My son and I spent many hours here. When he was young he played with toy soldiers at my feet. I would re-enact Hysteria's ancient battles, and Auvlin showed me how he would fight when he was king. I knew he modelled himself on Mersium, but I did not mind – Mersium cuts a more heroic figure than me.' Janus looked back at Edwin. 'My, my – you look every inch the royal prince.' He gestured to the door. 'Shall we go?'

They walked along the passage and Janus took Edwin's arm. 'Now – I have some news – Hercula returned to court this afternoon. As you know she was close to Auvlin, so you must be particularly careful in her company.'

'Right,' Edwin said, suddenly terrified. This was the kind of thing Ollwin couldn't teach him. 'How ... what were they like together?'

'Almost like brother and sister – affectionate, playful. She may take you by surprise!'

'Is that why she doesn't know Auvlin died?'

'Yes, she has lost every member of her own family ... Auvlin's death may be too much for her to bear so soon.'

Edwin listened to the level tone of the king's voice. Janus was so calm, but there was so much to remember. Edwin tried to think of something – anything – that Ollwin had taught him. He came to a sudden stop.

'What if I mess this up!' he blurted. 'At home I'm no good at anything. My dad always reads my report last ... my little brother never asks me to help with his homework. Now I've got to learn all this stuff – all these names and dates, and who my mother was and how much she loved me ...' Edwin's bottom lip trembled. 'You all think I can do it, but no one's asked me!'

Janus sighed. 'Forgive me, Edwin. I see you are still lacking confidence. You cannot see what we see – what I see – an intelligent and courageous young man. Intelligence comes in many forms and not all of them are measured by tests and the acquisition of knowledge. Your manner puts people at ease, you are loyal and determined and you always strive to do what is right. There are many learned men and women who do not possess these qualities.'

Edwin bit his lip. 'So you think I'll be all right?'

'Yes, I do.' Janus smiled. 'Do you feel ready to go?'

Edwin nodded, and it seemed no time at all until they met Perpetua and Ollwin outside the Great Hall. Eifus and Dreifus were standing to one side, adjusting identical robes. Neither fitted properly.

'Dear departed mother would be so proud!' Dreifus cried. 'Do you remember, brother dear, our outfits when we were young men? Matching tunics, matching tights, matching shoes. No wonder no-one could tell us apart!'

Eifus approached Edwin. 'I understand you are also fully prepared for tonight, my friend. Do remember dining etiquette – manners maketh the man!'

Dreifus beamed. 'You will be a most convincing prince. Have you any experience in the art of acting?'

'Er ... I played a cow in a school production of Calamity Jane.'

Perpetua coughed. 'That's a musical show very popular with cowboys and geriatrics.'

'Ah! Then you will overcome any first-night nerves. And you, my lady – have you experience on the stage?'

'I had to get an award in assembly, for best performance in science.'

Edwin creased his nose. 'I don't think that counts.'

Ollwin clapped his hands. 'Take your places. Edwin, remember you are royalty. Take your time and people will wait – do not be afraid to think before you speak. Good luck!'

A gong rang out. Edwin took a shaky breath and jammed on his crown; best it was secure – it wouldn't take much to turn him into a gibbering idiot. At least when he played the cow he hadn't had any lines.

The doors swung open and a chattering hiss shrank to silence. Edwin followed Janus, and as they passed through the arch he craned his neck to see hundreds of people, all straining to catch a glimpse ...

The gong thundered again, then a voice boomed, 'Stand and hail King Janus the Eighty-Third! Stand and hail Auvlin the Scion Prince!' There was a moment's silence before Edwin came into proper view, then, suddenly, a burst of applause.

'Hail well, Auvlin!' a single voice cried.

'Warm greetings, young prince!' cried another, then the air was filled with noise.

Edwin gave his best regal nod and kept walking, dragging against the weight of his costume. They reached a long top table, and Janus took his seat with Edwin and Perpetua on either side. The crowd were still cheering, but the noise died down as Janus clasped Edwin's hand and raised it.

'Today, my beloved son returns to court. Join our celebration!'

Applause erupted again. Janus glanced at Edwin, and Edwin tipped his head to the crowd.

'You will now greet our Privy Council,' said the king quietly.

Three men and one woman walked forward; Edwin had seen portraits of them, but he still glanced down at the notes on the back of his hand. Ridiccia – tall. Dissius – well ugly. Perwin – chubby cheeks. Merion – big nose.

Edwin looked up as a hand reached out for his.

'Prince Auvlin, it is a pleasure to see you again.'

'Thank you, Lord Ridiccia.'

'Praise be – a miracle if ever there was one!'

'Indeed, Lord Dissius.'

'How happy we are that you are returned to good health.'

'I am grateful, Lady Perwin.'

'May you go on to a long and happy reign.'

'Thank you, Lord Merion.'

'Well done!' Janus whispered as the four shuffled away. 'Now for the ambassadors.' He stood up to speak, but a voice suddenly yelled, 'Where is Lord Mersium?'

Silence descended for a few seconds.

'Hear, hear! Is there news of him?'

Janus's jaw hardened. 'We still hope to find Mersium – that is all I have to say.' He cleared his throat. 'Prince Auvlin will now meet the ambassadors.'

A line of men and women stood up, but their footsteps were drowned by a swell of murmurs. Then, 'Where is Lord Mersium?' echoed across the hall again.

Edwin shifted in his seat. Why were they asking the same question? Had they heard something, some rumour? What should he do?

Without thinking, Edwin stood up and shouted, 'My father is right – our dearest wish is for Mersium's safe return!'

There was silence, then a smattering of applause. Edwin shook all the ambassadors' hands, then he looked at Janus. The king stared back long and hard, making Edwin swallow. Had he put his foot in it? Had he said the wrong thing?

But Janus's gaze softened. 'That, my boy,' he said, 'was exactly what Auvlin would have done ...'

Edwin was relieved when the formalities were over, and soon the tables were crammed with food. Apart from the hog-trotter pie, it all looked pretty splendid. Platters of roasted meats and vegetables sat amongst tureens of exotic fruit and vanilla and hazelnut cakes perched on sparkling crystal stands. Edwin's mouth watered like Niagara Falls. Why couldn't they serve this sort of stuff every day? He was just planning his next move, when he glimpsed a figure hovering behind Janus.

'Your Majesty,' said a soft voice.

Janus's face brightened. 'Hercula!'

Edwin twisted in his chair. A young woman stood before him; a sheet of long black hair flowed onto a simple white dress, and bright blue eyes glittered with excitement. Primus stood nearby, gazing at her.

Hercula smiled. 'Are you well, Auvlin? Are you recovered?'

Edwin stood up, and for a moment Hercula seemed taken aback by his height. But then she smiled, and her pale face was so open, so friendly and warm, Edwin didn't feel hesitant or awkward, as he usually would with a stranger. 'Yes, Hercula.'

'That is marvellous!' she cried, throwing her arms around him. 'I have so much to tell you ... I have met so many interesting young ladies! May I see you first thing tomorrow?'

Edwin looked to Janus. 'Er, Father ...?'

Janus took Hercula's hand. 'All in good time, my dear. Auvlin will need to rest in the morning. And you have to settle back into your rooms.'

Hercula hesitated, then looked behind her. Malita stood some way back, mumbling and wringing her hands. It was funny – to Edwin she didn't look at all scary now.

'How long will it take to unpack my things?' Hercula said.

'A morning and a night ... or a night and a morning,' Malita replied.

Edwin noticed Perpetua sit up. He caught her eye and mouthed, 'Nutter.'

'Auvlin can see you when you are settled,' Janus said. 'We have many years to find our young prince a bride.'

Edwin raised his eyebrows. They could take as long as they liked. 'I will ... er, see you presently,' he said, stumbling to find the right tone.

'As you wish,' Hercula said brightly. She leant down and kissed Janus's hand. 'It is so good to be back at court!'

Edwin watched as Primus walked Hercula back to her seat.

'That was Malita, wasn't it?' Perpetua whispered to him across Janus's back.

'Didn't you recognize the old bat?'

'Yes, but ... oh, I'll tell you later.'

Janus turned to Edwin and grasped his hand. 'You should be very proud, my boy, you have exceeded all our expectations.'

Edwin felt his stomach flip. 'I wanted to do well,' he murmured. 'I wanted to do well for you.'

Janus's fingers squeezed his, and Edwin looked into the king's eyes. Was he proud of him too? As they stared at each other, Edwin saw no pride. What he saw, what he felt begin to flood over him, was so, so much more.

CHAPTER NINE

THERE WERE NO LESSONS the next day. Edwin was quite happy to lie dozing in Perpetua's room, mentioning every now and again how pleased Janus had been with him. At first Perpetua agreed enthusiastically, but by the eighth time she said 'Yep' through slightly gritted teeth. She went off in a huff, came back with Bellwin and announced it was time to practise his apprentice tasks. It was only after Edwin had tuned-in to the servants bickering over the washing-up, that Perpetua remembered something.

'You know when we did this the first time, when I heard someone talking? Well, I worked out who it was.'

'You did?' said Edwin.

'Yes – I heard the voice again, at the banquet. It was Malita.'

Edwin was intrigued. 'Was it? That beats a tiff about who'll wash and who'll dry …'

'What was it I heard her say?' Perpetua said vaguely. That's it – it grows steadily ... then, the work is nearly done.' She shrugged. 'Maybe she's got a runner bean plant on the go.'

Edwin huffed. 'The woman's right offer trolley! I'm surprised the bouncers let her into the banquet.'

Bellwin looked at Perpetua.

'Bouncers,' she repeated. 'Well-built men who guard night dubs or pubs to keep out undesirables – you know, the sort who might start a fight.'

'Night clubs ... pubs?'

Edwin nodded. 'Places where people – mostly adults – meet up to drink alcohol and dance to ... to music.'

Perpetua smirked. 'Which you didn't fully explain the last time it came up!'

Edwin looked at Bellwin. 'D'you want me to try again?'

'Is it important?'

'Nah ...'

There was a collective sigh of relief.

'I've been thinking about the banquet,' Perpetua said. 'People were asking about

Mersium, and it made the king look very uncomfortable.'

'Ollwin says there are rumours, but Janus's spies still have no definite sightings of Mersium,' Bellwin replied. 'The king is bound to worry what has happened to him.'

'What are the rumours?' Edwin asked, his stomach tingling.

'Ollwin would not tell me.'

'But where could Mersium have gone?' Perpetua said. 'Did he have any favourite places – somewhere he might've escaped to?'

'He did sometimes take leave from the castle, but where he went I do not know.'

'So who might know? If only we had a few ideas ... it would do Janus such good to get his friend back.'

Edwin's mouth twitched. 'Yeah,' he said nervously, 'it would.'

There was light tap on the door. 'May I come in?' said a soft voice, and Hercula appeared. 'Good day, Auvlin … Bellwin. Good day, Lady Perpetua – how are you?'

Perpetua stood up. 'Fine, thank you.'

Hercula took her hand and shook it vigorously. 'I forgot to introduce myself at the banquet. And you looked so pretty! I have not been to the eastern lands -you must tell me about them. I hear you are very learned ... we have so much in common!'

Edwin blinked. If Hercula tried really hard, he was sure she could squeeze in a few more compliments. She turned to him with a beaming smile.

'Auvlin, we need to discuss prospective brides. Can I see you this afternoon, alone?'

'Yeah … er, yes. After lunch?'

'That will suit me very well I can take my archery lesson before we meet. May I come to your room?'

'Of course.'

'Thank you! As I said before, I have so much to tell you! Good morning, everyone – so lovely to meet you, Perpetua!'

Hercula rushed out, and Perpetua raised an eyebrow. 'Isn't she the jolly type?'

'She's full-on,' Edwin agreed. 'If she was at Temp Grove Comp she'd definitely captain the hockey team. I hope she doesn't talk me into anything silly – I am just a boy, after all. Bellwin, what passes for a royal bride around here?'

Bellwin stroked his chin. 'The heavier the better, with a large nose and ruddy complexion.' He winked at Perpetua. 'And they must bathe at least once a month.'

'Fabulous!' she trilled. 'Just what the wizard ordered – sounds like you'll be dating Miss Piggy!'

Edwin watched them both giggle. There was no need for translation.

Edwin struggled to keep awake after lunch. He'd eaten far too much as he tried to ignore Perpetua's prediction that Templeton Grove would soon have another Mrs Spencer. (Edwin had shuddered. If he ever got married, he'd change his name.) He opened his wardrobe in search of entertainment, and grunted at the sight of tunics and pointed leather shoes. He was sick of being dressed for a pantomime!

Edwin grabbed his school uniform and held it up. That was more like it – trousers and a blazer, all in black! Edwin ran his arms into the blazer, stepped in front of the minor and snorted at the sight. It was way too small. There was no point trying on the trousers – they'd look like an end of August panic-buy. He'd just hung the blazer over the back of a chair, when Hercula appeared at the door.

'We will start straightaway,' she said, taking a seat. She sorted through a pile of papers. 'Now, this lady first – she is sixteen, a little older than you, but she is a talented artist and is fluent in many languages.'

She could speak ancient Swahili for all Edwin cared. 'Anyone else?'

'Isobell of Meticulla. She is a very attractive young lady. She would like to wait at least four years before marrying, but that would not prevent a promise of betrothal.'

Edwin winced. Over his dead body. He had to admit, from the drawing she was quite pretty, but she had shoulders like an all-in wrestler. 'Very nice. But, er ... not what I had in mind.' He looked at Hercula's wad of papers. He had to make lots of excuses, but he wasn't going to run out ...

An hour later, Hercula sighed, 'Are there any here you like?'
'Well ...'
'Never mind – I cannot expect to find your wife at my first attempt! And, like Janus, you must marry for love.' Hercula stood up, then said, 'I have something in my shoe ...' She reached out for Edwin's chair to steady herself, and her hand rested on his blazer.

Hercula looked at it and hesitated. Edwin held his breath. Then Hercula pulled the blazer from the back of the chair 'What is this, Auvlin – a garment? What a strange emblem Temple ... Templeton Grove. What is that?'

Edwin sprang to his feet. This was bad enough ... what if she noticed the distinctly non-Hysterian biro in the inside pocket?

'It's er ...' he mumbled, his thoughts fogging. Why hadn't he put it away?

Hercula peered at him. 'Yes?'

'It's a type of cloak! Primus brought it to court ... from the eastern lands.' What a masterstroke! Hercula had never been there.

'I see.' Hercula held the blazer up. 'Then Lady Perpetua would be familiar with it?'

'Oh, yes,' Edwin said, nodding violently. 'Very.'

Hercula hung the blazer back on the chair. 'How interesting! Now, I must visit the library so I can read about the eastern lands before I talk to Perpetua.'

'Why not!'

'Goodbye ...' Hercula said cheerfully, and she disappeared.

Edwin put his blazer on its hanger and shoved it back in the wardrobe, out of sight. He'd better find Perpetua so she could get swotting up on the eastern lands before Hercula beat her to it. Just as he approached the door it burst open, and Perpetua and Bellwin bundled in.

'Has she gone?' Perpetua hissed, but she didn't wait for an answer. 'I think we're onto something!'

'The Court Record!' Bellwin cried. 'If Mersium was attacked, and fled fearing for his life, he may have gone to a familiar place. The record shows where people went when they were away from Court – it may give us clues of where to search for him.'

'We can go to the library now – before dinner,' Perpetua added.

Edwin followed them reluctantly into the passage. Did they have to go hunting for Mersium? Did they have to go looking for trouble?

Once again, the maze of dusty shelves was a people-free zone. In addition to Worst Kept Library, the award for Most Infrequent Lender could also have been up for grabs.

Perpetua led the way. 'It's here,' she said as they rounded a corner. 'At the –'

But the Court Record wasn't there. Perpetua looked up, then down. 'Where's it gone?'

'It is not the sort of book to be borrowed,' Bellwin said. 'We will find it somewhere.'

By the time they'd scoured the library, they were covered from head to foot in dust.

Perpetua fended off a sneeze. 'I can't believe I didn't think of this before, Bellwin, but why don't you use the finding charm?'

Bellwin blew his nose, then got to work. An orb appeared straightaway. 'Well done!' Perpetua whispered. 'Let's see where it takes us.'

The orb began to move. It circled for a few seconds, as if it were gathering its bearings, then it suddenly darted right. Edwin scurried after it, followed by the others. He expected the orb to shoot off again any second, but shelf after shelf whizzed by. Very soon they were going to run out ...

And they did. The orb approached the library door, slipped to the top and squeezed through a gap.

'It's going outside,' Edwin gasped. 'Bellwin, I thought –'

'I know ... quick!'

They flew through the door then stopped, glancing from side to side.

'There it is!' Perpetua shrieked, and Edwin and Bellwin rushed after her.

Away from the library the orb slowed, shining much brighter than the others Bellwin had conjured. 'Ollwin would be pleased,' he said, 'if I could tell him.'

They followed the orb for quite a way. They seemed to be heading downwards.

'Where d'you think it's going?' Perpetua said.

But no one knew.

The stone beneath their feet was now quite damp. The orb's glow intensified, then it suddenly took off. 'Quickly,' Perpetua hissed, 'it's gone down there!'

Narrow stone stairs wound down into pitch black. Edwin went first, feeling his way for each shallow ridge. After countless steps he stopped dead.

'What's the matter?' Perpetua said. 'We'll lose the orb!'

'There's a door ...' Edwin fumbled for the handle and the door creaked open. He stepped into another dank passageway. Edwin frowned, sure that he'd been here before. Except, last time he'd come from the opposite direction ...

'The orb!' Bellwin cried.

Edwin felt the others push past him as he tried to get his bearings. Where was he?

A torch on the wall suddenly sprang to life. By its side was an arched wooden door, surrounded by carved stone flowers. Edwin felt the pit of his stomach drop as the orb floated to the top of the door and disappeared.

It had brought them to the mausoleum.

CHAPTER TEN

EDWIN'S FACE TURNED WHITE. 'What's the record doing in there?'

'Bellwin, what does this mean?' Perpetua whispered. 'Could the king –'

'No – Janus did not want to see that book ever again.' 'But he's the only one who can get into the mausoleum. He holds the key.'

'Lorius had it,' Edwin whispered, 'when he showed us inside.'

'Only because Janus lent it to him,' Perpetua hissed. 'Other than that day, Janus never lets the key out of his sight. He's hardly going to give it to any Tom, Dick or Harry ... and certainly not so they could take the record into the mausoleum, where Janus might see it.'

'Couldn't Lorius have sneaked the book in when –?'

'Of course not' Perpetua replied impatiently. 'We looked at the record the day after we'd seen Auvlin's body.'

Edwin scratched his head as he tried to work it out. 'Why would someone take a book like that in there?'

They'd been so deep in conversation, they hadn't heard footsteps approach. A deep voice suddenly said, 'Which book – and in where?'

They spun around. Lorius stood there. 'Which book?' he repeated.

Perpetua was the first to think on her feet. 'A book of spells!' she blurted. We're trying to guess what Bellwin's final task will be. The book's somewhere in the library.'

'We've been helping Bellwin practise his tasks,' Edwin added. 'We kept it secret 'cos we've used some magic.' Edwin knew that might get Bellwin into trouble, but it seemed better than saying that they were snooping around.

Lorius glowered, his gaze passing from one to the next. 'Come with me – all of you!'

The three exchanged looks, but no one moved.

'I am waiting,' Lorius said slowly. He watched Edwin take the first step, then turned on his heel to lead the way.

Edwin was furiously trying to think of excuses as they walked into the throne room. Silence descended. The courtiers who had met them that first day in Hysteria were there but no one else was around. Ollwin was beside the throne, his head cast down in thought. Primus stood stony-faced, his hands gripping the helm of his sword. Janus was pale and drawn, but his eyes prickled with anxiety.

'This looks bad,' Edwin whispered. Bellwin looked almost frozen with fear.

'News has come to me this morning,' Janus announced. 'And it has grave consequences for all of us.'

Hang on, Edwin thought, this might not be about being caught downstairs ...

'My worst fears have been realized,' Janus continued. 'My spies report Mersium is alive ... within the Umbrian fort.'

Edwin stared at the king. For a second it didn't register what he'd said. 'Umbria?' Edwin whispered, trying to steady himself. 'What ... what's Mersium doing there?'

'We are not sure, but I do not think it is of his own free will.'

Edwin glanced anxiously at Perpetua – Janus didn't seem to know anything for sure.

'I … I know Mersium's your friend,' Edwin croaked. 'But could he be on their side?'

'No,' Primus growled. 'Impossible!'

Lorius coughed. 'Either way, it seems information about our defences is now in Umbrian hands ... but again, it is not dear if Mersium has given this willingly.'

'And what does that mean for Hysteria?' Edwin said quickly.

Janus met Edwin's gaze in silence. Edwin tried to guess what was coming …

'That the Umbrians may be planning to attack,' Janus said.

'They will,' Primus added. 'General Aquilla's greatest ambition is to conquer Hysteria for Hereticus.'

Edwin's eyes widened. He couldn't believe what he was hearing. 'But Your Majesty, you ... you said Hysteria would be safe as long as the Umbrians thought you had an heir.'

Janus looked down. 'No longer, it seems ...'

Something inside Edwin ignited. They'd said he'd be safe, too ...

Perpetua took Edwin's arm. 'Your Majesty,' she said calmly, 'so your spies don't know how Mersium got to be in the fort?'

Janus hesitated. 'We only know that he is within its walls.'

'Mersium is surely being held by force,' Ollwin added, 'and if he has given away secrets, it would only be under the influence of Shadow Magic.'

Edwin guffawed. How could they know that? What if Mersium had been spying for the Umbrians all these years?

The Umbrians will continue to use magic,' Primus said darkly. 'We must rescue our friend before it is too late – for him and for us.'

Janus raised his hand. 'But there is something else, Edwin – the rescue of Mersium must be considered an act of defence, which is where Hysterian tradition must be observed. Centuries ago our Privy Council decreed that any such act should be led by a member of its royal family ...'

Janus faltered and Edwin stopped breathing. If he didn't know better, the king was about to ...

'I am weak,' Janus said. 'I would eagerly take my troops ...'

'What are you saying?' Edwin whispered.

'That you must lead the rescue of Mersium,' Primus said bluntly.

Edwin's jaw almost hit the ground. Yeah, he thought then I'll build the Taj Mahal out of lolly sticks.

'You're kidding,' he grunted. 'Me – lead troops?'

'Yes,' said Primus, clutching his sword, his face flushed with excitement. 'The Umbrians would see for themselves that their attempt on Auvlin's life has failed. Hysteria will seem even stronger!'

Perpetua was suddenly beside Edwin. 'Don't listen to him,' she hissed. 'They can't make you go ... they can't make you.'

'Too right!' Edwin looked at Janus. 'I can't believe you're asking me to do this. You promised I'd be safe, and now you want me to go to war ... and rescue Mersium! I know you don't think he killed Auvlin, but nobody knows for sure!' He put his hands to his head and felt his temples throb. 'You're asking for all this, and I don't even come from this stupid place! And d'you know what I've never asked – what do I get out of this what's Hysteria ever done for me?'

Edwin waited for someone to answer. Was this the best they could do – couldn't they even think of an excuse?

'Nothing,' Janus replied quietly. 'It is we that ask everything of you.'

'Well, Your Majesty, that's just not fair!' Perpetua said tartly.

Primus turned to her. 'What would you have us do?' he snapped. 'Leave our kingdom undefended?'

Bellwin sidled up to Edwin. 'Do you think Lorius will tell on us?' he whispered.

Edwin screwed up his eyes. Why couldn't they all shut up ... he was trying to think.'

'Look – this rescue mission,' he shouted, and suddenly there was silence. 'What would it involve?'

Janus looked up. 'Primus will take my private guard and spring a surprise attack.'

'So there might not be any real fighting?' Edwin said hopefully.

'Not if the attack goes to plan,' Primus answered. 'Although you would be seen as our leader, I will be in command,' he paused. 'I would give my life to protect you, Edwin.'

The passion in Primus's eyes nearly made Edwin say "yes" on the spot. He looked at Janus. Could he even begin to understand how much this man needed to help his friend, Mersium? The old feelings of shame swept over Edwin. Yes, of course he could. Edwin would do anything to turn back time to that playground fight …

'I ... I need to think about it.'

'WHAT!' Perpetua shrieked. 'You're not seriously –'

'I'm not saying I'll do it yet' Edwin interrupted.

We will need an answer soon,' Ollwin said. 'By tomorrow morning.'

'That soon! Can't you give me a bit more time?'

'No – the King's Guard will be ready to leave by the afternoon.'

Perpetua swished her skirt. 'You can't expect Edwin to take a risk like that without –'

'Don't speak for me!' Edwin cut in again. 'They're not asking you to go.'

'Good job,' Perpetua trilled, 'because I wouldn't even consider it!'

Janus stood up. 'Please, Perpetua – I know you are concerned, but we will do our best to protect your friend.' He put his hands on Edwin's shoulders. 'You will feel the answer in your heart. It must be your decision.'

'All right,' Edwin said firmly. 'But if I say yes, there's a condition – I'll help rescue Mersium, but as soon as the vortex has enough power I want to go home.'

Janus closed his eyes, and a lump caught in Edwin's throat.

'I like being here ... with you,' he whispered. 'But my life is somewhere else. That's the deal – Perpetua and I go home together.'

'If that is what you want, my boy, that is what you shall have.' Janus leant forward and kissed Edwin's forehead. Edwin's gaze followed the king as he walked from the room. He'd never seen him look so lonely.

It was well past midnight, and Edwin sat slumped at his table. One moment he'd convinced himself that Janus was right – Mersium was innocent, and Edwin should lead the charge to rescue him. But the next, Edwin was racked by doubt. What if they were wrong? What if the moment Mersium thought he saw Auvlin, he drew his sword?

Edwin had ended up getting his blazer out of hiding again. Now he stared at the badge thinking about home. Nat was strong, Nat was confident – what would he do?

It was useless trying to guess. Would Nat feel the same warmth for Janus that Edwin felt? Edwin swung the blazer over his shoulders and huddled into its lining If all this had never happened, it'd still fit him ...

The latch on Edwin's door suddenly sprang up. Edwin got to his feet and shook off the blazer. Hercula appeared and put a finger to her lips.

'Auvlin,' she murmured, 'I am sorry to disturb you. I must be quick – the court is thick with suspicion and I must not be found here.'

'Hercula, what is it?'

She took a deep breath. 'Janus has told me everything ... Mersium is within the Umbrian fort and he has asked you and Primus to rescue him.'

Edwin didn't say anything. He wasn't sure Hercula should be talking about this

'I am not here to argue whether you should go,' Hercula added. 'But I know you are not fully recovered from the attack, and I can offer something that may make your decision easier.' She opened her hand and tipped a gold chain into Edwin's palm. A small charm nestled amongst the glittering coils. 'This is the Amathan Amulet.'

The amulet was made of tarnished metal. Words were inscribed around its circular edge, but the letters were tiny and hard to make out. As the amulet sat in his hand, Edwin was sure it warmed his skin.

'It is very powerful,' Hercula went on. 'It belonged to my father. The writing is a language of a bygone kingdom.'

'What does it do?'

'Whoever wears it is protected from injury and death, so it is highly prized. It was one of the pieces the Umbrians sought when they ... when they came to my father's house.'

Edwin frowned. 'So how come you have it?'

'My father had shown me the amulet only minutes before our house was invaded, and when I made my escape it came with me. I have always believed it saved my life. No one knows that I have this, Auvlin ... it would be sought again by any means.'

'No one knows – not even Janus?' Edwin suddenly realized he should have said. 'Father, but Hercula seemed not to notice.

'No one. Janus would not take it from me, of course, but the fewer who know it is in my possession the better.' Hercula grasped Edwin's hand. 'But now I must take a risk – if you lead the expedition to rescue Mersium, I want you to wear the amulet. I have lost all my family, and I could not bear to lose you, too. Let the amulet protect you as it did me. Will you wear it for me ... please?'

Edwin stared at Hercula. Was she thinking about her younger brother, he wondered, killed in front of her?

'Yes ... of course I will.'

Tears gathered in Hercula's eyes. 'Thank you ... you will not regret it. Now, I must go – I have already been here too long.' She stood up. 'You look tired, Auvlin – you should go to bed.'

'But I can't sleep ...' Edwin replied.

'You must try,' Hercula said softly and smiled. 'Perhaps you should sing yourself a lullaby ...'

Hercula opened the door, then the latch clicked closed. A lullaby? Edwin didn't think they had music here? But then again, her job did take her to all sorts of places.

Edwin blinked and held the amulet up to the light. Hercula must be very fond of Auvlin to risk giving him this Very fond indeed.

CHAPTER ELEVEN

THE NEXT MORNING, EDWIN had made up his mind about the rescue mission. The amulet still lay hidden away, but its presence gave him confidence, and he found himself striding towards the Throne Room with a determination he'd never felt before. He arrived to find everyone assembled and the king looking well; his face had a touch more colour, and the rings under his eyes were not quite so dark.

'Good morning, Edwin,' said Janus. 'I hope you did not sleep badly.'

'I did all right, Your Majesty.'

'Very good. It is strange – I too slept deeply and for many hours ... probably for too long, as this morning my head does not feel quite as it should. After yesterday's discussions, I thought I would lie awake, but one cannot always anticipate the body's reactions, Janus paused. 'Have you come to a decision?'

All eyes were on Edwin. There was barely a breath to be heard. 'Yes,' he said simply. 'I'll go.'

'OH ... MY ... GOD!' Perpetua's face was almost purple. 'What are you doing? You can't go on this expedition! What if you're injured ... what if you're killed?'

Edwin felt calm He felt in control. 'I won't be.'

'You don't know that!' Perpetua wailed. 'This is too much of a risk!'

'Primus has promised to look after me ...'

Perpetua put her hands on her hips. 'I know you trust him,' she sighed. 'Primus is strong and brave, but he's just a man. Look, I do understand ...'

Edwin walked to Perpetua and put his arms around her, and he felt her ding onto him. 'Trust me,' he said. 'I'll be all right. And while I'm away they'll get the vortex working ... next minute you'll be sitting in the science lab with all your notes.' Then, he whispered, 'Who d'you reckon school'll get in next – Count Dracula?'

Perpetua looked up, blinking away what might have been tears. 'D'you think I'm staying here without you? No way – if you're going on this expedition, I'm coming too!'

'It's a good job we had those riding lessons,' Perpetua said through clenched teeth.

It was the middle of the afternoon and they were almost ready to go. Perpetua sat on a fat grey pony. Her back was as rigid as a broomstick and her hands held the reins like a string of best sausages.

'Yeah,' said Edwin. 'You, er ... look really confident.'

Perpetua closed her eyes. 'Edwin,' she croaked, 'are we doing the right thing?'

Edwin couldn't answer that, so instead he looked around the courtyard. Primus was saddling his black stallion and supplies were being ferried into a wagon. Ollwin suddenly appeared and hurried over the cobbles to speak to Primus.

'Psst!' Edwin heard, and looked down to see Bellwin. 'I'm coming with you!'

'Fantastic!' Edwin cried. 'How come?'

'Ollwin is joining the expedition – we may need to fight magic with magic ...'

Edwin grimaced. He didn't like the sound of that.

'... but my birthday is in fourteen days, and Ollwin must witness my next two apprentice tasks. So I must follow him!'

As Primus signalled they were ready to leave, a door swung open and Janus appeared. He walked to where the horses were standing and bowed to Primus, Ollwin and Bellwin, then turned to Perpetua.

'Dear Lady, your bravery is astonishing. Please promise me one thing – you will stay close to Primus. His promise of protection extends to you.'

Janus walked to Edwin's horse, and ran his hand along its side. 'Good Honaris,' he murmured, finally rubbing the stallion's nose. 'You will look after my boy, I am sure.' The horse snorted, and Janus smiled. 'Ah ... you can tell. No matter, I know you will protect our guest.'

Janus looked up and grasped Edwin's hand. 'Hysteria owes you a greater debt that I had anticipated. Good luck! My heart goes with you.'

Suddenly, Edwin felt scared – but not for himself. Who would protect the king while they were away? Who would look after this kind and noble man?

'You'll be safe here, won't you?' Edwin asked.

'Of course, my boy,' Janus replied.

The gates swung open and Primus kicked his horse forward. As the others followed, Edwin turned to look at the king.

'Goodbye,' he yelled. 'I'll see you soon ...' His gaze didn't flinch until Janus had disappeared from sight.

They passed into the outer courtyard and a regiment of mounted troops came into view. Primus's horse led a path through the middle and the men saluted. They were young, with hard, proud faces and every one looked as brave as their commander.

Ollwin's horse trotted level with Honaris.

'Our expedition leaves Emporium Castle in good heart!' he cried. 'We will ride until nightfall, then set up camp on Hysteria's border. We have preparations to make!'

The castle's main gates opened. 'Ride ahead of Primus,' Ollwin shouted to Edwin. 'Give your people something to cheer. Bow, wave ... but most of all, smile!'

A sea of faces came into view and a roar went up. Honaris didn't flinch, but kept trotting smartly over the cobbles. The crowd was ten or twelve deep. It surged forward, everyone jostling to catch a view of Edwin. They were smiling, laughing, cheering. Edwin couldn't help but smile back. He waved and the roar increased; a ripple of euphoria washed over him. He waved again and the crowed yelled for more. Men threw their caps in the air and children were held aloft, their squeals drowned by a chorus of cries.

'Hail, Prince Auvlin!'

'Good luck to you, sir.'

'Hysteria is proud!'

'Thank you!' Edwin yelled, barely able to hear himself. 'Thank you ... goodbye!'

It was almost a mile before the crowd dried up. At the very end a little girl ran to Honaris and handed Edwin a small bunch of flowers. She grinned and touched his hand, and Edwin wanted to pull her up into the saddle. The flowers were tied up with coarse grey string, and only a few blooms sat bobbing amongst the rough green leaves. But Edwin tucked the posy into a buttonhole – the little girl wanted him to wear it.

Primus smiled at Edwin. 'Petris flowers,' he said, 'for good luck. They last six or seven days without water.'

'Wicked!' Edwin said.

'He means that's marvellous,' Perpetua added flatly.

Edwin touched the delicate purple flowers and made a wish. He wanted to get back to Janus before they lost their colour. Then, suddenly, Edwin realized he had more responsibility than just helping to find Mersium. He may not be the king's son, but he knew that if he didn't survive, Janus's heart would break a little more.

The sun was beginning to set. Ahead, the mountains that bordered the Wanchai Deserts could still be seen, but the white glow of their peaks had faded.

'It is time to make our camp,' Ollwin called. Tents flew up by the dozen, and Edwin, Perpetua and Bellwin soon sat around a blazing fire, watching a bubbling cauldron. Once the troops had settled Primus and Ollwin joined them.

'Let us eat,' Ollwin said as he unpacked five bowls. 'And we will discuss our plans for tomorrow. Stag and vegetable soup?'

The group sat in a semi-circle and huddled over their meal.

'Now,' Ollwin began, 'about the preparations I spoke of earlier: if magic has been used to make Mersium co-operate with the Umbrian, it will need to be reversed to make his rescue easier. So we must discover if any spells have been cast on him.'

Perpetua stopped eating. 'Can you do that?'

'Yes, at a place known as the Cave of Spells. It is hidden in the Balgarian Mountains, just half a day's ride from here. Every spell ever cast has a source of energy – a kind of soul. These energies rest in the cave, and contain the content of the charm and the name of the one who cast it.'

Edwin shrugged. 'So we just walk in and find out?'

'Alas, it is not quite that simple,' Ollwin smiled ruefully. 'The cave is minded by a witch called the Dorian Hag. She is the only living thing that may read these energies.'

'But it is hard to reach her,' Primus added. 'The caves are guarded by some kind of creature. Few men have come away with their lives.'

'But we've got all these troops – surely they'll manage?'

Ollwin shook his head. 'There are rules to be observed. Only two people may challenge the guard – the hag can see

224

outside the caves, and she picks those whom the guard will fight. One of those she chooses must appear the most capable and brave.'

Edwin's face fell. 'And the other?'

'The hag does not want anyone to reach the cave – her other choice will be the one who appears the least able.'

Edwin glanced around. That was, er ... him. 'So they could be a complete waste of space?' he said. 'Can she tell what happened in anyone's last fight?'

'She decides purely on appearance,' Ollwin replied. 'Do not worry, Edwin – we will try to keep you out of sight.'

'Of course, she might pick me,' Perpetua said in small voice. Edwin raised an eyebrow – he reckoned Perpetua might be pretty handy in a fight.

'We will see,' Ollwin said lightly. 'Once we reach the Dorian Hag she is obliged to read one spell only – but that should suffice. Anyone for more soup?'

Once dinner was finished they were quick to get to bed. As Edwin took off his tunic he noticed his petris flowers had

225

died. He groaned with disappointment. Primus had said they'd last for ages. But Edwin put them aside: all that mattered was that he got his wish and got back to Janus.

The night air was cold, so it was good to snuggle into fleecy sleeping bags. Edwin lay in between Bellwin and Perpetua, and Primus lay across the tent opening with his sword by his side. With a full stomach, Edwin dozed off the moment he rested his head.

'Wake up!'

Edwin came round with a jolt, clutching the amulet. Perpetua was sitting up, hair strewn over her face.

'Wake up!' she repeated. 'You're dreaming!'

'Sorry ...' Edwin rubbed his eyes. 'Did I disturb your brainy sleep? Don't worry – you couldn't get any cleverer.'

'You were muttering and mumbling for ages. What were you dreaming about?'

Edwin tried to think. 'I ... I was walking through this dark corridor, and there was this funny smell. Then I was in a room – it was pitch black, but somehow I could still see ... I could feel what was in there ...'

'Too much soup!' Perpetua hissed, and she lay down with a huff. But within a few minutes she was snoring.

Edwin rolled over and reached for the amulet again. It was a strange notion, but had he been dreaming about Umbria?

The next morning was bright and clear. Primus rose first, and made a breakfast of bread and soft cheese. Edwin still felt half-asleep as he ate, and it wasn't until Ollwin joined them that he really woke up.

'How did you all sleep?' Ollwin asked as he packed away the plates.

'Not bad,' Perpetua said, shooting a snotty look at Edwin.

'You were snoring all night,' he said.

'But at least I didn't babble!'

Edwin ignored Perpetua and sat next to Ollwin. 'You know Hereticus, the Umbrian leader?' he said. 'Does he live at their fort?'

'It is thought so. But remember, he has not been sighted for over two years.'

'Is there any chance we'll come across him?'

Primus looked up. 'Not if our attack goes to plan. We need to slip into the castle, take Mersium with the least possible resistance, then escape.'

Perpetua frowned at Edwin. 'Why are you asking about Hereticus?'

Edwin stopped to think. It had to be that dream – it had been so dear. That in itself was weird – normally he never remembered them.

'Dunno,' Edwin said dismissively. 'Just curious, I s'pose.'

Ollwin threw a sack over his shoulder. 'Let us concentrate on one thing at a time. We have a difficult task in front of us today. Come, my friends – our horses are ready for us!'

The Balgarian Mountains loomed large, rising up from a wide plain. They stood as four peaks, and the ground leading up to them had risen steadily for two or three miles. A member of the guard suddenly appeared ahead in the gorge, riding towards Primus and Edwin through a swirl of fine dust.

'I have found the mountain entrance to the cave!' he shouted.

'How far?' Primus yelled.

'No more than an hour, my lord, in a clearing – it lies beneath a black overhanging rock.'

Edwin, Perpetua and Bellwin didn't talk as they rode further along the rocky path. The mountains towered over them, huge stone crags jutting at every angle. It took only the slightest sound to cast an echo and shadows flickered behind every rock. Eventually they came to a small clearing.

'We are here,' Primus bellowed, reining in his mount.

Ollwin's horse trotted forward.

'How shall we approach the cave?' Primus asked Ollwin. 'And where can Edwin and Perpetua keep out of sight?'

'About twenty kilometres away,' Edwin said under his breath.

'There is a crevice over there,' Ollwin said. 'Edwin ... Perpetua … Bellwin – come with me ... steer your horses into the shadows before the hag is aware of our presence.'

Primus waited for all his troops to file into the clearing, and soon he had organized them in two lines with him standing alone behind them Edwin, Perpetua and Bellwin hid in the shadows but could still see everything clearly. The cave entrance was huge, but there was nothing to be seen inside except deep pitch black. Edwin shifted in his saddle and looked across the dusty clearing. After the monotonous pounding of hooves, it was all very quiet.

They waited. After a while Edwin looked at Ollwin, then across to Primus, but they were both staring resolutely ahead. The troops and their mounts were still and silent, only the occasional pound of a horse's hoof breaking their formation.

Suddenly, a streak of light whizzed from the cave. It shot up like a rocket, then hovered for five or six seconds.

'What's that?' Perpetua said, craning her neck.

'It is the hag's eye in the form of an orb,' Ollwin replied. 'She is about to make her choice.'

The orb swooped down and ran along the first line of the King's Guard. It doubled back along the next, racing a few inches from the soldiers' faces. It didn't pause once and in no time had reached the last one. Without hesitation, it raced over to Primus and stopped a few inches from his face. It hovered like a giant firefly then buzzed against his cheek.

'She has chosen the bravest,' Ollwin said. 'And now ...'

The orb shot up into the sky again and circled the formation of soldiers.

'The hag is thinking,' Ollwin added nervously. Suddenly, the orb flashed towards the shadowy crevice.

'It's seen us!' Perpetua hissed.

The orb flew into the half-light, then hovered: Ollwin ... Perpetua ... Bellwin ...

The orb darted to Edwin and bounced off his nose. He blinked, took in three stuttering breaths then let out an enormous sneeze.

'I noo it!' Edwin said snottily. 'I noo she'd bick me!'

'No – she can't,' Perpetua cried. 'She chose you over me ... and I'm a girl!'

But the orb had already gone, streaking inside before Edwin could even find a tissue.

'Shall we give the hag a bit more time?' he mumbled, then looked at Perpetua. 'I don't want you to go in, but that soldier over there is shorter than me ... shall we get him to flex his muscles?'

'I'm sorry it's not me,' Perpetua said indignantly. 'It's not only Primus that wants to protect you, Edwin. I do too.'

Edwin stared at Perpetua, then put his arm around her shoulder. Who would've thought it?

'The hag has chosen Edwin,' Ollwin said gravely. 'She will not change her mind.'

Primus rode over; his hand was already on his sword. 'It seems we will fight the hag together Edwin. Do not worry – we will both survive the Cave of Spells.'

Edwin swallowed. If what Hercula had said about the amulet was true, he knew he would. But Primus might be hurt ... or even killed. And what would happen if Edwin was left alone – would he ever see the light of day again?

CHAPTER TWELVE

AN HOUR LATER EDWIN STOOD with Primus at the mouth of the cave. He looked down and bent his knees. Considering this was someone else's armour, it was a very good fit.

'Whose stuff is this, then?'

'It belonged to Auvlin,' said Primus bluntly.

Ah, of course. 'He ... he wasn't wearing this when ...?'

'No. If he had he would still be alive, and you would not be here.'

This didn't make Edwin feel any better. Primus had only been able to guess what was in the cave, waiting for them.

'Are you nervous?' Edwin said shakily.

'No. Try to stay calm – you are well protected. Are you ready?'

Edwin glanced into the darkness. 'Yeah,' he squeaked. 'We can't put it off forever.'

Primus led Edwin inside, picking his way through scattered rubble. The roof of the cave was low, and they both had to duck around shards of damp black rock. Primus pointed ahead to a burning torch.

'This must be the path.'

They worked their way towards the glow. From somewhere there was a drip, drip, drip of water.

'Where d'you think the guard is?' Edwin whispered.

'Deeper into the mountain.'

Further in the air was more humid. The rubble became thicker and walking was more difficult. Edwin felt his heart pump. Primus reached the torch and pointed to another narrow cave that rose steeply to the left, this time lit as far as the eye could see.

'This way.'

Edwin followed, a musty smell drifting into his nostrils, his hand clammy on the hilt of his sword. He passed unlit alcoves, holding his breath as he crept by. He wouldn't know if anything was in there until it was too late.

By the time they reached the top, sweat was running down Edwin's back. They met a curved passage that was higher and wider than the last. Primus bent down and touched ridges of brown dust.

'These look like wheel tracks,' he murmured.

At that moment there was a low rumble. Edwin and Primus looked up, holding their breath as the noise fell away.

'What was that?' Edwin whispered.

Primus glanced left then right. 'I do not know. Follow me.'

Edwin and Primus walked stride for stride, each scouring the shadows all around. Their footsteps kicked up clouds of dust, and Edwin tried not to cough. He was trying to listen for the slightest sound of life ...

Primus suddenly stopped dead and pointed to a shaft of light. He and Edwin ran forward then skidded to a halt, staring up at a hole in the rock. There was the roof of another cave and the light inside it was very bright.

'This must be the Cave of Spells,' Primus said.

'Great!' Edwin whispered. 'And we haven't even seen the –'

Rumbling came from way down the passage. This time the sound was clear – it was a slow, grating trundle of wheels.

Primus stepped back and drew his sword. The noise grew, then sped up to a noisy clatter. Edwin fumbled for his sword but his fingers trembled around its hilt. A shadow slid along the curve of the passage and a huge form burst into view.

'Move!' Primus yelled.

Edwin fell to one side, just catching sight of something flash by. The floor shook and dust spun in the air. The rumbling receded as Edwin staggered to his feet.

'What was it?'

'The guard.' Primus looked at the brightly lit cave. 'Can you climb up – before it returns?'

Edwin looked down at his armour. 'I can try,' he croaked. Primus hauled him up and Edwin lurched onto a shallow step, fumbling for somewhere to put his fingers.

'Look to the left,' Primus gasped.

Edwin grabbed a lump of rock. 'Where now?'

'The ridge above your head.'

There was another faint clatter and Primus hoisted Edwin onto his shoulder. 'Hurry!'

Edwin stood on his toes and groped around, but he couldn't find anything. The noise grew louder. Edwin's stomach lurched and he scrambled up. The stone began to crumble and Primus took Edwin's weight.

'Climb up!'

Edwin tugged against the rock, his fingertips sliding over the smooth damp stone. The walls began to shake and Edwin turned to see something rush along the track ...

A large wooden chariot sped towards them. Two huge wheels thundered over the dust, with a pointed shard of metal spinning in their centre. The creature in it stood nine or ten feet tall – a giant with a bulldog neck and bulbous yellow eyes. Long muscular arms whipped the wheels forward, but Edwin's jaw dropped at the sight of another pair held out in front of the beast, sharp claws curving from thick fingers.

The giant craned his neck, focusing on Edwin. The chariot raced forward and the giant raised a hand.

'Keep still,' Primus yelled, stepping away. Edwin's legs buckled as Primus raised his sword.

The rumble grew to a deafening crescendo. Edwin closed his eyes. Something swished towards his head and he heard a scraping of claw on metal. Edwin looked down. Primus's sword was smeared with red and the chariot raced away, the giant's forearm streaming with blood.

Edwin's eyes widened. The giant wasn't standing in the chariot: it was ... it was part of it! Its body was growing out of the centre, the wood and flesh blending into one. Edwin felt saliva flood into his mouth – he was going to be sick ...

'Get down!' Primus shouted.

By the time Edwin recovered, the giant had appeared again. The gargoyle face peered down the passage, its mouth stretched into a wide primeval snarl.

The beast's lower arms slowly turned the wheels as the upper limbs placed two spears by its side and lay another in its palm Edwin squinted and saw that the chariot wheels were textured – shards of wood mixed with wrinkled flesh. They looked very hard, like rhinoceros horn.

'Have you seen what that thing's made of?' Edwin said weakly.

'Not now!' Primus snapped, unbuckling his shield. 'Kneel down – he is about to aim.'

There was a gurgled grunt and something thrust through the air.

CLANG!

Primus's body shuddered and a spear clattered sideways.

CLUNK!

Another spear smashed into the shield and fell at Primus's feet.

'One more,' he said. 'He is losing patience …'

The giant let out a savage roar and the last spear whistled harmlessly past and out of sight. Primus picked up one of the others.

'Keep behind me and do as I say.'

Edwin looked down the passage. The giant was staring at them, then it started to roll the chariot forward. Primus pointed the spear towards the ground.

Edwin said, 'Shouldn't you point it up?'

'No!' Primus snarled. 'Just stay behind me!'

The chariot gained pace, the wheels speeding towards them Primus stood as if ready to pounce. The chariot sped closer but Primus didn't flinch Edwin began to panic – when would Primus take aim? A few more seconds and it would be too late ...

Point it up, he mouthed. Point it up ...

Primus didn't move. Edwin reached to launch the spear. The creature roared. His eyes bulged and spit spilled onto his lips. He was almost on top of them ...

'POINT IT UP!'

Primus threw the spear downwards just as Edwin lunged forward, but Primus leapt to shield him. The spear clattered into the chariot's right wheel and there was a thunderous crack. The wheel's spokes smashed in quick succession as wood splintered in mid-air. The cart lurched and bounced, then tumbled over and over like a spinning baton. The floor shuddered and there was a deafening crash.

Then, silence. A cloud of dust rose and Edwin stood up. Primus was already on his feet. 'Wait' he said.

Gradually the air cleared. Piles of mangled wood lay twisted along the passage, debris scattered as far as the eye could see. On the other side of the cart lay the giant, its head smashed and bloody.

'Is it dead?' Edwin whispered. Grisly as it was, it was hard to tear his eyes from the glistening red flesh above the giant's ear.

Primus picked up his sword and shield. He climbed over the debris, flinching as shards of wood cracked under his feet but the giant didn't stir. Primus stopped within a few metres of the body and began to kneel down.

A sudden roar ripped through the air. The giant rose from the wreckage and tore its torso from its wooden base. It lunged forward, pulling at Primus's sword.

'NO!' Edwin picked up a rock and threw it. It bounced off the giant's arm and the beast turned, scouring the ground. It picked up a rock and held it aloft, glaring at Edwin. As it drew back its hand, it released Primus's sword from the other. Primus lunged forward and thrust the blade into the giant's neck.

The giant gurgled but it was still staring at Edwin, drawing its arm back further. Edwin ducked, buried his head in his hands and steeled himself for pain But nothing came There was only a long gasp and a dull thud.

Edwin looked up to see the giant lying in a crumpled heap.

'Is it dead?' he repeated, his voice still trembling.

Primus stepped over the body, gripped the hilt of his sword and pounded the blade down twice.

'Yes ...' As he withdrew the sword and held it up, blood streamed from the giant's neck. 'What were you doing, Edwin ... the giant almost killed you!'

'I ... I was trying to help,' Edwin replied vaguely. He was feeling kind of odd. Normally just the thought of blood made him feel queasy, but now he couldn't take his eyes from the pool collecting on the floor.

'You do not need to help,' Primus growled. 'I perform the heroics!'

'Sorry,' Edwin said. He looked up to meet Primus's stern gaze.

'We need you alive,' Primus added, sliding his sword into its sheath. 'Now, let us find the Dorian Hag.'

Primus pulled Edwin up through the cave entrance. He squinted and shaded his eyes from the bright light. This place was huge, even bigger than a football stadium. How could a mountain be this

244

hollow and not crumble? Edwin looked down. Four paths led away through craggy boulders and half-dead plants. Where did they go? Edwin blinked, lowered his hands ... then caught his breath.

The source of light was all around. Thousands of orbs shone from tiny pockets in the cavern walls like a sea of shimmering honeycomb. Up close each orb was distinct, but further away they merged so that the cavern's far end was lost in a dazzling glow.

Edwin's mouth gaped. He'd never seen anything so beautiful.

The sound of laboured breathing jolted his senses and he turned to see a shock of white hair rise from the gloom of the dust track.

'Wretched adventurers ... why do they shift and shake the walls?'

The small figure of an old woman scaled the rock and pulled her twisted body into the light. She stood up, shook her tunic and gagged on a gruff cough.

'What do you want with the Dorian Hag?' she yelled. 'Who disturbs my sleep?'

The hag's eyes were large and wide-set, their whites no more than an off-grey. Her face was covered in green boils, festering in her nostrils and the corners of her mouth, and her lips turned down in a purple slash.

Edwin grimaced. He'd never seen anything so ugly.

'Who disturbs my sleep?' the hag repeated, spitting saliva onto her chin. 'You have no business here.'

Edwin stepped forward. 'Yes we do. I'm ... I'm Prince Auvlin of Hysteria. And this is Primus, my father's First Knight.'

The Hag's eyes narrowed at Primus. 'It was you who killed my faithful guard,' she screeched. 'Where do you expect me to find another?'

'I understood you had to choose the bravest opponent,' Primus replied quietly. 'Am I not to your liking?'

The Hag huffed. 'If I had my way I would choose only the weakest ... I am made uglier each time an adventurer reaches this cave.'

Primus examined the hilt of his sword. 'Then you must ensure your guard is better trained, madam.'

Edwin winced; if Primus pushed his luck any further he'd break the world record. He cleared his throat. 'We want to ask about a spell that was cast on one of our friends.'

'And you think I will help you?'

'You must help us,' Primus growled, gripping the hilt of his sword. 'We have reached the Cave of Spells, so have earned the reading of a charm.'

The hag eyed Primus's hand. 'Very well, but I am obliged to give one reading only.' She jerked her head. 'Follow me,' she grunted, and shuffled towards the centre of the cavern. 'Who is your friend?'

'Mersium Sijeanus,' said Primus.

'And when was the spell cast?'

Edwin looked at Primus. 'Would there have been more than one?' he whispered.

'Ollwin said we should ask for the very last spell cast on Mersium,' Primus replied. 'He is sure it will be the one we need.'

After a few minutes a marble table came into view. The Dorian Hag walked around it and stopped. 'Well, when was the spell cast?'

'We do not know,' Primus said. 'But we seek the last one used.'

The hag's gaze flicked down and she circled her fingers on the marble, as if she were digesting Primus's words. 'Mersium Sijeanus,' she murmured, and closed her eyes.

She was silent for two or three minutes. At first she stood with her brow furrowed. Then the corners of her mouth creased with a faint smile, and she suddenly jumped up and down.

Edwin didn't like the look of this and he whispered, 'What's she up to?'

At last the hag opened her eyes. She guffawed, then let out a loud cackle.

'Well?' Edwin said anxiously. 'What d'you have for us?'

The Dorian Hag clapped her hands. 'Nothing, good Prince Auvlin,' she squealed. 'Nothing at all!'

'Nothing ... what d'you mean?'

The hag wiped away a tear. 'There have been no spells cast upon Mersium Sijeanus.'

'I don't believe you. You saw something ... I know you did.'

'Yes,' the hag admitted. 'There is a charm, but Mersium Sijeanus was not its subject. It was cast on one of his possessions. And as you have not asked me to read that spell, I am not obliged to help you.' She laughed. 'May I show you the way out?'

Primus looked at Edwin. 'We must find something,' he growled.

'Yeah. You never know ... that spell might help us.'

Primus narrowed his eyes at the hag. 'You have given us nothing, madam – we demand you read this other spell!'

'Demand! You are entitled to one request and you have made it.'

Primus dragged his sword from its sheath. 'We cannot leave empty-handed. If need be, your blood will also be smeared on this blade!'

The hag stepped back, raising her hands. Wait! I can give you clues, but nothing more. And you cannot harm me – I have not acted against Ancient Magical Law.'

Edwin pulled at Primus's arm. 'Look,' he whispered. 'I know you're all fired-up, but you should calm down a bit. Shouldn't we just do this and get out of here?'

Primus looked at Edwin then nodded. Once he'd lowered his blade, the hag closed her eyes. She placed her palms back on the table and whispered, 'Mersium Sijeanus ... spell elaborata.'

A golden orb rose from the marble, hovered for a few seconds then shot high in the air. It paused, its light intensified, then it sped towards one side of the cavern.

'Where's it going?' Edwin asked.

'For the soul of the charm,' the hag replied sulkily.

The orb stopped and hovered a few feet from the cave wall, then a tiny flicker of light melted into it. The orb dimmed then shot back towards the table. It dived, the Dorian Hag opened her mouth and the orb flashed inside, hissing as she shut her lips.

Primus gripped Edwin's arm. 'Listen carefully – we must remember everything.'

The hag opened her eyes to reveal bright white light beaming through the sockets like car headlights. Her lips moved silently, as if she were processing words and digits. Her body convulsed, she retched in a gulp of air, then opened her mouth.

'Hear me well,' she began. {'The creator's ear will take his sight, a timeworn book long stays their hand. The low will take a groundless flight, where the mile is neither clay nor sand.'}

The Hag shuddered, screwed up her eyes, coughed and regurgitated the orb. It sank into the marble, leaving behind a puddle of thick yellow spit.

Edwin looked at Primus. 'It's a riddle.'

'Yes. And we will not waste time asking this miserable wretch to tell us its meaning!'

The hag wiped her mouth with the back of her hand. 'Now you have learnt something, my lord, I demand you leave my cave!'

They didn't need a second invitation. Primus tipped his head then strode down the dusty track. Edwin followed and as he scrambled down the stone wall, he began to recite the riddle over and over again. He had to remember it; he had to get it right. A short while later he picked his way towards daylight, and his frantic whispers had slowed to a steady stream of words.

They emerged into sun's rays, blinking. Ollwin ran towards them

'Edwin! Primus! Are you hurt?'

'We're fine!' Edwin yelled. 'JUST GET ME SOME PAPER!'

The camp had settled for the night, and once again they were gathered around a blazing fire. Ollwin looked intently at a piece of script. 'Now – this spell was cast upon one of Mersium's possessions, but it is still worth pursuing.'

'Can you think which possession it might be?' Perpetua asked.

'Where would we start? We do not even know when the spell was cast. But we have the riddle – we should go through it line by line.'

Perpetua took the lead straight away. '"The creator's ear will take his sight, "' she read. 'It could mean someone is going blind, but who can it be?'

'Someone who has created something,' Edwin replied. 'Could it be an inventor, or a writer ... or even some sort of god?'

'No, Edwin,' Ollwin said hopefully. 'I think I have something! This could refer to the creator of Mersium's spell.' He pointed to the second line. 'That would make sense of "A timeworn book long stays their hand". All wizards are bound by the book of Ancient Magical Law.'

'All white wizards, master,' Bellwin said. 'Which would mean that ...'

253

Ollwin nodded. 'The spell would not have been cast by anyone practising Shadow Magic.' He sighed. 'However, the Umbrian could still have been involved – they have forced many worthy wizards to help them over the centuries.'

'So what about the ear bit?' said Perpetua.

Ollwin smiled. 'That will require more thought, my dear. But we have made such progress in only a few minutes, I am certain it will not be long before the entire riddle is solved!'

The fire had gone out, its blackened logs glowing only the softest orange. Edwin yawned and wrapped his cloak tight around him. Perpetua pinched herself awake.

'Can't we look at the first line again?' she whined. 'We're not making any progress at all on where the wizard lives.'

'No,' Ollwin said firmly. 'Rouse yourself, my friends – we do not sleep until we know tomorrow's destination.'

Edwin groaned and scratched his head.

'"Where the mile is neither clay nor sand,"' Primus read. 'This must hold some sort of clue.'

Edwin yawned again, but began to scratch letters in the dirt with a stick.

'What could be a mile long?' said Perpetua. 'Walls, ditches, a forest ...'

Edwin wrote MILE, ILEM, LIEM ...

'I do not think it would be something that obvious,' Ollwin said. 'Perhaps –'

Edwin sat up. 'No ... it's not a mile.'

Perpetua snorted. 'That's what is says here.'

'Look!' Edwin pointed at the last word he'd traced. 'It's lime – an anagram of mile. Lime is neither clay nor sand!'

'Meticulla!' Ollwin cried. 'Its soil is predominantly lime!'

'Could that be the place we're looking for?'

'Yes, indeed I did my apprenticeship with two or three Meticullans, and they all went on to become fine practitioners of magic. Well done, Edwin!'

The more Edwin tried not to look at Perpetua, the more his gaze was drawn.

She stared into the middle-distance with SECOND FIDDLE written all over her face. She glanced back at Edwin for a nanosecond and grunted, 'Yes, well done.'

Primus stood up. 'It will take no more than a day to ride to Meticulla. Once we have found our wizard, we can start our journey to Umbria before nightfall tomorrow.'

'How long will it take to get there?' Edwin asked eagerly. 'Can we do it in one go?'

Ollwin raised his eyebrows. 'Your impatience to see Umbria surprises me, my friend.'

Edwin shrugged, but Ollwin was right. Although there was everything to be afraid of in Umbria, Edwin couldn't wait to get there.

'Now,' Ollwin added, 'we all need a good night's sleep.' He winked at Edwin. 'Particularly those who deserve it!'

Perpetua snorted, got to her feet and flounced over to her tent. 'Bully for them,' she blurted. 'The rest of us can toss and turn all night!'

Edwin looked at Bellwin. 'She's used to coming first ... maybe being a brain-box isn't all it's cracked up to be when someone knocks you off your perch.'

The tent suddenly flew open and Perpetua's head popped out. 'He means it's not as good as you might think,' she hissed. She retreated, then looked out again, and added, 'And a perch is where a bird sits!' The zip ripped down.

Edwin waited ten minutes before he eased the zip back up, and found Perpetua snoring. He quickly settled, but couldn't sleep for a while. His thoughts kept returning to the sight of the giant's blood streaming from its neck.

Edwin shook his head, trying to put it out of his mind. He wanted to sleep – they had a big day tomorrow. He fumbled under his tunic for Hercula's amulet and closed his eyes.

They'd been riding since before dawn when Perpetua suddenly let out an ear-splitting shriek.

'HEY! I've solved it!'

She kicked her pony to a trot and bounced over like a baby in a bumper car.

'Solved what?' Edwin said flatly. 'The common cold ... world hunger ... how to ride a horse like a space hopper?'

Perpetua yanked hair from her mouth. 'That's a child's inflatable bouncing toy,' she said to Bellwin. 'Now, the riddle's first line – we've been thinking about the creator's vision. But I think it's about hearing – the creator takes his sight to lip read.'

Edwin sat up. 'You mean the creator could be –'

'Deaf! Ollwin, what d'you think?'

'You could be right. And there cannot be many deaf wizards to choose from in Meticulla.' Ollwin's eyes brightened. 'I have a book in my study that lists all white wizards – it includes information about where they live.'

Edwin frowned. Either he was missing something, or they'd left the castle two days ago. 'Great ... but won't you have to send one of the soldiers back to get it?'

'No. I have a very useful tool which enables me to look through any of my books, even if they are many miles away.'

'Oh, yes!' Perpetua cried. 'We read about it!'

Ollwin looked at Bellwin. 'Did you remember to pack the reading stone?'

'I think I saw it, but ...'

Ollwin glowered. 'I suggest you pray you see it again when we arrive at Meticulla. If not, you will return home no closer to Full Wizarding than when you left!'

'I ... I will find it, master,' Bellwin stammered, and let his horse slip back.

The sun came out for the first time that morning and Edwin squinted. The light seemed brighter than yesterday. He tugged the brim of his hat. Maybe his eyes were tired?

'How long till we get to Meticulla?' he said. 'I'd like to get into some shade.'

Two of Primus's men unpacked Ollwin's things, and a dozen sacks were spread under a tree. Bellwin flitted between them. 'I am sure I put it in this one.'

Ollwin stood stony-faced. 'I would wager all my money you cannot find the reading stone. But we could use this opportunity to perform an apprentice task.'

Bellwin shot up. 'Now, master? Solaris locatio?'

'Of course! Which other charm would you use?'

'None other, but this is so important, I –'

'It is probably against my better judgment,' Ollwin said. 'But if you do not succeed I will do it myself. Now, stand amongst the sacks.'

Bellwin shuffled to the left and shoved his hands in his pockets. He looked like the new boy at school. 'Solaris locatio,' he winced, and screwed up his eyes.

Edwin held his breath, willing Bellwin to succeed. By the time his throat began to press for air, there was still nothing.

'Shut your eyes first,' Ollwin said. 'Take your hands from your pockets, and speak clearly!'

Bellwin linked his fingers, closed his eyes and shouted, 'SOLARIS LOCATIO!'

Edwin shielded his eyes against the sunlight. It was hard to see, but after a few agonising seconds an orb glowed above Bellwin's head.

'It has appeared,' Ollwin said quickly. 'Concentrate your thoughts on the stone.'

The orb began to drop, and Bellwin sank to his knees. It floated delicately then drifted towards an open bag. The orb paused, then plopped inside. Bellwin yelped and dived in. He threw out rags and boxes, bottles and cups, scattering trinkets everywhere. Finally he sighed and held up a small grey stone.

Edwin clenched his fists, did an imaginary high-five and danced a mental jig. He glanced at Perpetua. She smiled serenely. No doubt she'd ticked the box marked Apprentice Task Ten, and was planning her next move.

'I knew it was in there,' Bellwin said.

Ollwin whipped the stone away. 'That is a matter for debate ... but well done. Perhaps we will find time for the next task before we return to Hysteria. Now, I must look at my Index of Wizards – you should watch with the utmost care.'

The others gathered round as Ollwin placed the reading stone in his palm, blew on it twice and closed his fingers. 'Concentrate, Bellwin – my hand is not too tight ... the stone's auras are able to escape.' Almost at once yellow smoke trickled out. 'My Index of Wizards,' Ollwin said, and opened his hand.

Masses of smoke billowed out, swirling into a miniature cloud. Gradually the centre of the haze cleared to show a book, then lines of text were visible, sharp as ink on paper. Index of Wizards, said a heading and below it was a large letter A.

Ollwin looked into the circle. 'Find the letter M.' The pages flicked all the way to

Z. 'The alphabet has never been this spell's forte,' Ollwin added lightly.

Finally, the book fell open at M. 'Over,' Ollwin instructed, and the book flipped one page. 'Over ... over ... stop!'

Edwin could see three place names in bold type. METICULLA was the last.

'There it is!' Perpetua cried. 'What a lot of names. Are they all wizards – will it say which of them are deaf?'

'Yes, my dear,' said Ollwin. 'It gives a wealth of information.'

'And will it say exactly where they live?'

'It will give a location within the kingdom – but that should be enough. Ah, this is promising. "Hildeguard Brolin ... an experienced wizard who specializes in spells on inanimate objects. Seventy-two years old. He holds daily consultations in his home, although visitors should be aware he has become hard of hearing in recent years". Perfect! According to this, he resides in Spartandine Valley.'

Primus summoned one of his men. 'How long to ride to Spartandine Valley?'

'Only a few hours, my lord.'

'Then we will reach it within daylight,' Ollwin said. He waved his hand, and the smoke shrank back into the reading stone with a high-pitched whistle.

'That's a very clever toy,' Edwin said wistfully, thinking of his last maths test. 'They'd cost a fortune back home.'

'It is invaluable to me.' Ollwin held the stone up. 'Bellwin, I want you to look after this. Keep it in a secure pocket.'

Bellwin took the stone and dropped it inside his cloak. 'I will not mislay it again.'

Ollwin clasped his stomach. 'We will eat then ride to Spartandine Valley. We have almost completed the second part of our quest. After this it will be onwards and upwards, to Umbria!'

To Edwin, 'Spartandine Valley' conjured up all sorts of images: a lush expanse of land, children dressed in white running through tall grass, dear blue skies and towering mountains. But what he found was a scrubby crevice divided by a muddy creek. The worst thing was, there wasn't a house in sight.

He'd expected to ride into a village and see Home of Hildeguard Brolin on a shiny plaque above a door. What were they supposed to do now?

'It doesn't look like anyone's ever lived here,' Perpetua moaned.

'This was given as Brolin's dwelling place,' Ollwin replied. 'So he must have been here once.'

'But what if he's not here now?' Edwin said. 'Can't we go straight to Umbria?'

'You're in a hurry,' Perpetua scoffed.

Ollwin took the script from inside his cloak. 'We have yet to solve the riddle's third line, remember? It may help us.'

Everyone crowded behind Ollwin, and Edwin let Perpetua push to the front.

'"The low must take a groundless flight,"' Edwin read over her shoulder. 'What are we talking about here – pygmies?'

Everyone looked at Perpetua. 'A very small breed of humans who live in Equatorial Africa,' she reeled off. She looked up. 'What about groundless flight – does that refer to a kind of bird?'

Edwin let Perpetua get on with it. He fed his horse then walked up the valley, looking for a sign of anything that might be a home. But he didn't see so much as a welcome mat, and by the time Edwin trudged back Bellwin had made lunch. It was in the middle of hog's buttock sandwiches that Primus sat up.

'Edwin, what was the word you spoke yesterday – when you changed lime to mile?'

'Anagram – it's called an anagram.'

'Could there be an anagram here? Low – could it be owl?'

Perpetua's eyes glinted. 'Oh, yes,' she cried. 'That would make much more sense!'

Edwin swallowed a crust. 'Ollwin,' he called. 'Get out your reading stone – Perpetua needs to look at Hysterian Bird-spotting for Beginners.'

Perpetua ignored him. 'The owl must make a groundless flight – let's look at that.'

'It could be wol,' Bellwin suggested. 'Does that fit?'

It didn't get any better. Perpetua tossed and turned the words so many times that even her head began to spin. After a while Primus lost patience and got up to stretch his legs. He'd just ducked under a tree when he suddenly spun around.

'It is low!' he said, striding back. He snatched the script from Perpetua. 'If something is groundless, it could be underneath the ground. And what might we do if we walk underground?'

The others' faces lit up, and they cried, 'KEEP LOW!'

Primus ordered his men to search the whole valley for any sign of an underground home. It took a bit of time, but eventually an eager soldier found a tunnel behind a clump of bushes Primus went in first, with Edwin behind him. Faint orbs in the ceiling shed some light, and at the end was a wooden door. A lopsided sign hung on the doorknob. On it was written, 'THE WIZARD IS IN'.

Edwin turned to Ollwin. 'That's a result.'

Ollwin reached for the doorknob, but it turned by itself and the door swung open.

Inside the room was small but brightly lit, and an old man sat behind a desk at the far wall. He was bent over papers, a feathered quill poised between elegant fingers. 'One moment, please ...'

The man scribbled on his papers, then put down his quill and picked up a shell from his desk and put it to his ear. There was a short slurp then a muffled pop, then the man removed his hand and said, 'Auditoria.' The shell came away but what had been inside it stayed put.

'Pardon the delay,' said the man, turning to the door. 'These snail remedies are quite the latest thing – I am deaf, and this spares me from lip-reading. Now, what may I do for my first visitors of the day?'

Ollwin took a step in. 'I beg your pardon, you are Wizard Brolin?'

'Yes.'

'I am very glad to meet you. My apologies – we did not mean to interrupt ...'

Brolin stood up, and the hem of a crumpled tunic dropped over his knobbly knees. That is quite all right. And you are …?'

'I am Wizard Ollwin, from the Court of Hysteria.'

Brolin hesitated, then his green eyes brightened and he hurriedly brushed crumbs from his robe. 'Oh, Wizard Ollwin,' he gushed, 'I had no idea …'

'Again, I apologize,' Ollwin said, 'we are so unexpected. May I introduce my companions?'

Brolin grabbed a shabby woollen hat and pulled it over his hair. 'Of course!'

Ollwin took Edwin's arm. 'This is Prince Auvlin, son of Janus the Eighty-Third.'

The angle of Brolin's head shifted, like an owl's, and his mouth twitched an on-off smile. 'Yes ... the look of royalty. It is unmistakable. Please forgive that I did not recognize you – I know little of life outside Meticulla.'

'No need to apologize,' Edwin replied. He grabbed Primus's arm. 'This is Primus – my father's First Knight.'

Brolin switched his stare. 'A warrior, of course, my lord. There must be many tales of your bravery.' His gaze settled on Bellwin and Perpetua and he smiled. 'And who are these young people?'

'Bellwin, my apprentice,' Ollwin said, 'and Lady Perpetua of the eastern lands, cousin to the Hysterian Royal family.'

There was another slurping sound, and Perpetua peered at the side of Brolin's head.

'It's ... it's moving around,' she groaned.

'The snail is in no discomfort,' Brolin declared. 'Quite the contrary – it finds its new home most warm and moist.' He chuckled. 'And the sensation is very ticklish!'

Perpetua gave a sudden shiver. 'I think I need to sit down ...'

Brolin clasped his hands. 'I am in such esteemed company,' he said wistfully. 'Although, Ollwin, I am a little confused. Mine is a meagre practice and I ... He leaned in and pursed his lips. 'What I am trying to say, my friend, is ... what can I do for you?'

They sat down and Ollwin got straight to the point. 'It is a delicate matter, concerning one of our courtiers – his name is Mersium Sijeanus.'

Brolin's expression was blank. 'Should I know the name?'

'The Dorian Hag told us you cast a spell on one of his possessions,' Edwin said.

'You have been to the cave of spells?' Brolin gasped. 'It is a miracle you came out alive! What does the Dorian Hag look like? I hear she can turn milk sour at twenty paces.'

'You wouldn't want her near your rice pudding,' Edwin said flatly.

Perpetua coughed. 'That's a grain-based dessert made with milk and butter.' She closed her eyes. 'Oh ... I'd love a bowl right now ...'

'It sounds delicious – do let me have the recipe!' Brolin gushed. Then he started, and looked at Ollwin. 'But if you have risked entry to the Cave of Spells, you must need my help urgently.'

'Yes,' Ollwin replied. 'We need to know your charm's content, and when it was cast.'

'Of course. Your courtier – what was his name again?'

Ollwin barely had time to reply before Brolin rushed out of the room. He was back within a minute and dumped a pile of journals on the table. 'Sijeanus,' he muttered, 'Mersium Sijeanus. Here we are – edition fifteen, page seventy-five.'

As Brolin sorted through his books, the pit of Edwin's stomach tightened. He looked around, but no one met his gaze. Would this moment change everything? If Brolin couldn't help them, would they still be able to reach Mersium in the Umbrian fort? Edwin tried to suppress a spark of relief. That would mean he didn't have to meet him, face-to-face.

Brolin ran a fingernail down a page, then paused. 'It was eighteen years ago …'

Edwin sighed. Maybe too long ago to help.

'An unusual request – not heard before or since.'

Probably not what they were after.

'A charm on one of his possessions.'

The hag had told them that.
'And it was cast in secret.'
They knew that already, too …
A chair scraped back and Bellwin sprang to his feet. 'Well?' he blurted. 'What was the spell?'
Brolin's gaze turned to Ollwin, his eyes glittering with recollection.
'One cast upon the dagger of Mersium Sijeanus ... so only his hand could wield it.'

CHAPTER THIRTEEN

THE COLOUR DRAINED FROM EDWIN'S FACE. Ollwin and Primus gazed at each other. Only Bellwin continued to stare at Brolin. 'No – that cannot be right ...'

Brolin nodded. 'It was designed to prohibit anyone but Mersium Sijeanus using his dagger – its metal recognized his body chemistry alone and would burn the flesh of anyone else.'

Edwin caught his breath. Lorius's scar ... the restricted passage. He tapped Brolin's arm. 'Does it say which dagger?'

Ollwin shook his head. 'Mersium used only the dagger his father gave him – it was the one relic he kept of his home.'

Edwin and Perpetua looked at each other. He knew exactly what she was thinking: was Lorius's burn from the dagger? If so, when did it happen? Before Auvlin's death, or after?

Perpetua grasped Edwin's arm. Her hands were trembling. 'What shall we do?' she whispered. 'Should we tell them ... should we go back to the castle?'

Edwin closed his eyes and tried to think straight. Mersium could still be the killer, but either way, they had to get him out of the Umbrian fort, and they were already halfway there. Edwin tried to compose himself and fumbled for the amulet. 'No,' he murmured to Perpetua. 'We carry on – if we let on now, it would make things worse.'

They all sat in silence until Ollwin got to his feet. The damage done by Mersium's dagger was at his own hand. Our mission is not one of rescue, but counter-espionage.'

Edwin bit his lip and glanced at Perpetua. They couldn't say anything unless they were absolutely sure – could they?

Primus's fist pounded the table. 'I do not believe it! Mersium spent twenty years serving Janus. He would not have turned against us.'

Ollwin raised his hand. 'Perhaps he was against us from the very start,

Primus – a spy planted within Hysteria's court. Who really knows what is in any man's heart?'

'But why have such a spell cast on your own dagger?' Bellwin asked.

No one had an answer until Primus said quietly, 'A few years ago, Mersium told me that Umbria put a price on his head when he defected to Hysteria. When Janus took him in he promised to protect him, but Mersium's imagination grew wild, and he mistrusted any new servants or courtiers. His greatest fear was that an unarmed stranger would use his own weapon against him. It seems he took precautions none of us knew about. Not even me.'

'But why did he keep the spell a secret?' Bellwin asked.

'Probably because of Janus's promise,' Ollwin replied. 'He did not want to offend the king. He loved Janus... or so it seemed.'

'Mersium did love the king,' Primus said bluntly. 'Do not doubt it.'

Brolin wrung his hands. 'I fear I have spoiled your plans,' he bleated.

'You did only what was asked of you,' Ollwin replied. 'And we are better prepared – we owe you a debt of thanks.'

Brolin smiled weakly as Edwin and the others followed Ollwin to the door. 'May I ask,' he said, 'where you are travelling now?'

'Umbria's fort,' Ollwin said. 'Mersium Sijeanus is there.'

'Umbria? I did not realize …'

'Yes, my friend. We must not delay – Hysteria's future is in peril.' Ollwin tipped his head. 'Thank you, once again …'

'WAIT!' Brolin sprang forward. 'Let me help you further! There is a short route between here and Umbria – many are not aware of it, but I can show you the way. If we travel through the night we will arrive at the border by morning. Are you planning a surprise attack?'

'Yes,' said Primus, 'and we have not seen any spies.'

'Then you must get to Umbria as quickly as you can!'

Ollwin turned to Primus. 'What do you think, my lord?'

'We must take every chance we have.'

'Very good!' Brolin threw open a cupboard door and a pair of grubby woollen socks fell out. 'I will leave a note for tomorrow's customers,' he muttered, pulling one on. 'How surprised they will be to see, "THE WIZARD IS OUT"!'

They'd been travelling all night, but as the horses plodded through drizzly rain Edwin was wide awake. They were dose to Umbria and, strangely, he felt more alert with every step. Ollwin, however, was exhausted – he'd performed an invigoration spell on himself but it hadn't worked, and Bellwin had had to do it for him.

They knew the border was near when they came to the Blind Forest. They waited while Brolin rode ahead, and after twenty minutes he came trotting back through the trees. 'Fortune is with you!' he said, jumping down. 'There are no Umbrian in the vicinity ... I have used a little magic to be sure. Now, I suggest you ride north through the forest – it will take less than an hour.' Brolin pulled off his woolly hat, and his hair stood on end like mangled pipe cleaners.

Perpetua caned her neck. 'Has, er … has that snail been in there all this time?'

'Of course! He snuggled in against the night air.' Brolin patted his ear. 'And I am sure the little fellow found something to eat!'

Perpetua closed her eyes. 'I think … that's a bit … too much … information …' she croaked.

Ollwin took Brolin's hand. 'Please accept our most grateful thanks. Your help has proved invaluable.'

'It has been a pleasure. Now, I must return – I have preparations to make for tomorrow's surgery.'

'Anything of interest?'

'Goblin warts ... never a pleasant experience.' Brolin wrinkled his nose and waved his hat over his head. 'Goodbye everyone – and good luck!'

Ollwin watched Brolin ride away, then turned to the forest. 'Well, well,' he said. 'Are we ready for Umbria, my friends?'

Perpetua looked at Edwin curiously. 'I think he is ...'

The only thing Edwin could hear as the Umbrian fort emerged through the thinning trees was the snapping of twigs underfoot. Was the thumping in his chest fear ... or excitement? He scoured the grey stone walls. What was inside ... he had to find out. Edwin glanced left and saw that Perpetua was pale and drawn. What was wrong with him – shouldn't he feel like that?

They stopped before the forest edge, and Primus disappeared for a few minutes. 'There are no guards,' he said when he came back. 'It is better than I expected – there are only barred windows at the base of the fort.' He chose his three best soldiers. 'Edwin, we must be seen to lead these men.'

'I understand,' Edwin said. 'How are we going to find Mersium?'

'We will try a spell that will focus on Mersium's voice,' Ollwin replied. 'We must hope he speaks for us.'

'I promised I'd stay with Primus, too,' Perpetua added. 'So I ought to come.'

'No, it is too dangerous,' Ollwin said firmly. 'You should stay here.'

'But a promise is a promise,' Perpetua hissed. 'And I gave this one to a king!' She looked at Bellwin. 'What are you doing?'

'I should go with Ollwin to watch him perform the spell.'

'Then I'm not going to be left behind!' Perpetua nudged Edwin. 'I won't worry if you won't.'

'Very well,' said Primus. He drew a small dagger from his tunic and handed it to Perpetua. 'Tuck this into your belt.'

'Goodness,' she whispered, but she did as she was told.

The group of eight crept through the line of trees at the back of the fort. They checked the way was dear, then hurried across a ditch. Edwin threw his shoulder against a wall. Fear was shivering through him, but he couldn't wait to get inside.

Primus brandished a metal tool and dug it into a window. He heaved, and in no time three bars lay on the grass. Primus glanced at Ollwin's protruding stomach. 'One more, I think …'

The last bar lurched out and Primus hauled himself through the window. Edwin followed him into a tunnel, and the strangely familiar smell of damp hit him straight away. The others climbed in, and a soldier lodged the bars back into the window.

They appeared to be in the fort's foundations, but Ollwin suggested they climb up further, where the spell would be more effective. They followed the tunnel and, to their surprise, found an open, dusty slope. Primus scrambled into the darkness with Edwin dose behind him. They emerged into some kind of basement. A single torch was flaming and an open doorway led to a set of stairs. Edwin peered up them. 'How come this isn't locked?'

Primus pushed past and crept up the steps. 'Luck is still with us. Stay here,' he murmured, and disappeared from sight.

As they stood there, waiting, Edwin's heart thumped in his ears. His toes and fingers were cold, but his chest felt strangely warm. He sniffed; there was definitely something familiar about the air. Something muted and dark flashed through his thoughts. He shook himself. It reminded him of a dream …

Primus re-appeared on the steps. 'The dungeons are on the next floor. You may cast your magic here, Ollwin.' He jumped down and stood in readiness for the spell.

Ollwin looked around hesitantly. 'You are sure there are no Umbrian near?'

'Yes,' Primus insisted. 'Act now – we have no time to lose!'

'Very well. Stand back, everyone. Tell me when you hear something, Primus – it should take little time' Ollwin closed his eyes, raised his hand and said, 'Vocalia tunetarium … Mersium Sijeanus.'

Primus stood tall. He took three long breaths, then blinked hard. 'I can hear nothing.'

Ollwin began to lower his hand, then paused. 'We will try a second time,' he said firmly. He took a deep gasp of air. 'Vocalia tunetarium ... Mersium Sijeanus.'

This time they waited for what seemed like an age. Primus screwed up his eyes as the seconds ticked by. 'Still nothing!' he said impatiently.

Ollwin stamped his foot. The spell is not working ... why I do not know! Bellwin – earlier, did the invigoration charm come easily to you?'

'Yes, master.'

'Then there is something wrong with my auras.' Ollwin sighed. 'I think, my boy, you may be able to try your penultimate task after all.'

Edwin looked at Perpetua. Had they done enough work with Bellwin – would all their practice come good? The orb had been one thing, but this was serious stuff now.

Ollwin clutched Bellwin's arm. 'Use a deep, resolute voice,' he instructed. 'You must focus entirely on the task.'

Bellwin stood with his feet apart and shoulders thrust back. He closed his eyes and raised his left hand, the muscles in his forearm straining. 'Vocalia tunetarium … Mersium Sijeanus,' he said loudly.

Primus stood stock still. Suddenly his fists clenched. 'I hear it. I can hear Mersium's voice!'

'Set the spell,' Ollwin said quickly.

'It is complete, master,' Bellwin whispered, and opened his eyes.

'Well done, my boy!' Ollwin cried. 'We will make a wizard of you yet!'

Primus turned to the door. 'Mersium's voice is weak,' he said, 'but I can follow it.' He bounded up the steps. 'This way ...'

Edwin and the others followed and stepped up into a dimly lit passage. Primus hesitated. 'I can hear his voice more clearly now.' He led the way past a line of empty cells. 'We must try the next floor …'

As Edwin climbed another flight of steps, his legs felt hollow and his chin began to shake. He knew his amulet would protect him, but he couldn't fight the panic flooding his veins. He caught his breath as he heard someone shouting. It was a tired voice – tired but angry – and as Primus crept upwards its echoes distorted wildly.

Then, nothing.

Primus put a finger to his lips. He walked softly towards a door with Edwin at his shoulder. They reached it in silence and Primus gestured for his men to stand ready. He reached out for a latch and gripped it. He glanced back to Edwin, then to Ollwin, then slowly lifted the latch from its cradle. It drew up smoothly. Metal clunked on the other side. Primus gave a gentle push and the door edged back.

The room was in semi-darkness. In the middle a man was bent double, his hands wedged under his legs. He moaned and sat up, his head wobbled back and his eyes opened.

The man jolted upright. His mouth gaped. He stretched out his arms and chains rattled from the floor, irons straining at his bloodied wrists.

'Auvlin,' he cried, his eyes suddenly flaming. 'Mercy ... Mercy ... it was ...'

Primus rushed in and sank to his knees. He gripped Mersium's head, staring wildly into his eyes. 'My friend! My friend! You are still one of us ...'

Edwin almost crumpled, but he steadied himself and took a few steps into the room. He closed his eyes. Mersium was innocent!

But what about Lorius? Did this mean that ...

Edwin jolted as the others rushed past. Ollwin pushed forward and knelt down. 'He seems almost delirious ... they must have drugged him.' He gripped Mersium's arm. 'Mersium, listen to me ... have the Umbrians hurt you?'

Suddenly the door slammed shut. Two torches burst into flame and the shadows shrank back.

'Not yet.'

CHAPTER FOURTEEN

EDWIN AND PERPETUA WHEELED AROUND. In an instant a dozen soldiers sprang forwards to seize Primus's men. There was the clash of metal on armour. Shouts and curses muddled into one as Edwin was jostled from side to side. Primus cried out and tried to reach for his sword but was bundled to the ground. There was a sudden silence, and Ollwin stood with a dagger to his neck.

'I would not advise you to brandish your weapons,' said a thin, reedy voice.

An elderly man stepped forward. He looked around, his beady eyes glittering. 'Wizard Ollwin, Lord Primus ... and Prince Auvlin.'

Edwin frowned. This wasn't in the plan. Part one: find Mersium. Part two: take him back to Janus ... Primus glowered. 'Aquilla, I should have recognized the foul stench of evil as yours.'

Mersium reached out to Primus. His chains scoured the red flesh of his wrists and he moaned. Primus shrugged off the guards and knelt down. 'Take comfort, Mersium,' he said softly. 'We have come to your rescue ... we know you did not harm Auvlin.'

Aquilla looked at Edwin. 'Indeed,' he purred, walking towards him. The pleasure was all ours.' Edwin noticed the yellow tinge of Aquilla's skin and the bloodshot glaze of his eyes.

Aquilla pressed a hand onto Edwin's stomach. 'Did we cause you much pain, Your Royal Highness? Have the scars healed?' His lip curled and he squeezed a vicious pinch into Edwin's flesh, then he turned to Primus. 'How good of you to walk into our trap, my lord.'

Edwin straightened up, wincing. It had all been too easy – how could they have been so stupid? 'You knew we were coming ... of course you did.'

Primus glared at Aquilla. 'How could you? We did not see a single one of your spies.'

'It was not necessary to shadow your expedition – your plans were made known to us in advance.'

'Liar!' Primus growled. 'Our court holds no traitors!'

Aquilla paused, his gaze flitting playfully between the Hysterian faces. 'Then how do we know this boy is an imposter ... and that the real heir to your kingdom's throne lies still and cold in Emporium Castle?'

Edwin's stomach lurched. Shock turned to anger and he lunged forward, tearing at Aquilla's cloak. 'Who is your spy? Who is it?' He waited – waited for Aquilla to say, Lorius.

Aquilla caught Edwin's wrist. Well, well ... the boy who cried when first presented with Janus's challenge is now an aggressor.' He pulled away. 'You will see your traitor for yourself when you arrive back at court. It will make events so much more ... interesting.'

'Do not rise to his words!' Primus barked. 'We must keep a clear head.' He looked slowly around. 'Where is your master, Aquilla? Does he hide behind his generals ... is he too cowardly to show himself?'

'Hereticus is not here ...'

'Our spies have not seen him in two years,' Primus said. 'Is your mighty leader dead?'

Aquilla's eyes flashed. 'Oh no,' he said quickly. 'He is very much alive – unlike your corpse of a prince.'

There was a few seconds of silence, then suddenly Ollwin began to mumble under his breath. Aquilla turned on him.

'Do not waste your time! We have rendered the power of Hysterian wizards useless within ten miles of the fort. Your pathetic chants will not work inside these walls.'

'Then just wait till we get out of here,' Edwin muttered.

Aquilla smirked. 'Anyone of importance will find themselves under heavy guard – they will barely be allowed to breathe, let alone anything else.' He glanced at Perpetua and Bellwin. 'You need not count yourself or your friends amongst that number.'

Perpetua stamped her foot. 'You won't beat Hysteria! You don't know what it's capable of!'

'I know all I need to, Lady Perpetua. And I have done from the very beginning. As Hysteria made its plans we made ours, and you followed both to the letter.'

Ollwin swallowed against the blade at his throat. 'What do you mean?'

'Whilst you were distracted with this imposter, it gave us time to put our plans into place.' Aquilla kicked Mersium's chains. 'We dealt with Prince Auvlin, then brought this wretch to Umbria because we knew it was only a matter of time before you would try to rescue him. Our plan was simple – lure out Hysteria's finest troops and key members of its court, then invade Hysteria and gain control of the childless King Janus.'

Ollwin's lips trembled. 'Hysteria invaded ... when?'

Within the last day. Its court is under our strict control.'

Edwin stood shaking. His hand itched to draw his sword, but his gaze kept straying to the dagger held at Ollwin's neck.

'But you will see all this for yourselves,' Aquilla added. 'Your carriages await.'

'And once we are there?' Primus said.

Aquilla threw up his hands. 'The entertainment will begin!'

Edwin, Perpetua and Bellwin were huddled together in a carriage, their feet shackled to the floor. No light had passed through the canvas for many hours, so Edwin was sure it couldn't be far to Emporium Castle. Bellwin had fallen asleep, but Edwin and Perpetua had been talking about Lorius. Now they were sure of Mersium's innocence, who other than Lorius could be Umbria's spy? But they still didn't have any proof ...

The carriage jolted sharply to one side and Bellwin opened his eyes. 'I am sorry,' he croaked. 'I fell asleep.'

'Don't worry,' Perpetua replied. 'Are you feeling all right?'

'Yes ...' Bellwin rubbed his eyes and sat up. 'I wonder how Master Ollwin is – I hope his auras are not damaged.'

'Hey, how come you were able to cast that spell inside the fort,' Edwin asked. 'Aquilla said they'd blocked the magic of all Hysterian Wizards.'

'Because I am not a wizard yet.' Bellwin said bleakly, 'only an apprentice.' He shook his head. 'Why did I not realize there was a spy at court?'

Perpetua glanced at Edwin. 'D'you have any idea who it is, Bellwin?' she asked carefully.

'No ... and I cannot bear to think about it.' Bellwin wrung his hands. The spy told the Umbrian we were coming, but how did Aquilla know exactly when we would arrive?'

'Dunno,' Edwin said. 'Maybe they just prepared themselves as soon as we left.'

'Oh, of course!' Perpetua said curtly. 'A dozen men spend the best part of three days hiding behind a door. I don't think so!' She flicked a strand of hair over her shoulder. They probably used Shadow Magic.'

Edwin fiddled with the buckle of his shoe. 'Bellwin,' he murmured eventually. 'What d'you think they're gonna do to Janus?'

Bellwin didn't answer straight away. Perpetua bit her lip, and Edwin felt his heart sink.

'I do not know,' Bellwin mumbled as he wiped away tears. 'If only I could –'

'Hold on,' Edwin said slowly. 'Didn't Aquilla say something about me crying?'

Bellwin looked down. 'I do not remember.'

'I do, word-for-word,' Perpetua replied. 'He said you'd cried when first presented with Janus's challenge.'

'That's it! And who would've told him about that?'

Perpetua frowned. 'Their spy, I suppose.'

'Right! And d'you know the only person I've cried in front of since this whole thing began?'

Perpetua's eyes widened. Edwin looked at Bellwin and said, 'Lorius.'

'What are you saying?' Bellwin snapped. 'That is impossible ... Lorius is a good man!'

Perpetua said softly, 'And there's something else. The scar on Lorius's hand – it could have come from Mersium's dagger.'

Edwin nodded. 'Perpetua remembers the scar being fairly new in September – that wasn't long after Auvlin was attacked.' He took a slow breath to control his thumping heart. 'Bellwin, you must have seen Lorius with an injury …'

'Yes – his hand was bandaged.'

'And when was that?'

'I ... I noticed it the day after Auvlin died. But Lorius said it was a cut – from a riding accident.' Bellwin gulped, then cried, 'But why would Lorius want to kill Auvlin?'

'I dunno,' Edwin said. 'But we do know this – Lorius took Mersium's dagger and hid it. We followed him one night ... he took it from under a flagstone in a passage that was out of bounds. Why would he keep that secret? Put it together with everything else, and it doesn't look good.'

Bellwin put his head in his hands, and Perpetua put her arm around him. 'Don't talk about it any more,' she whispered to Edwin. 'Leave it for now, eh?'

Edwin sat back and fumbled for the amulet trying to guess what they were about to walk into. Once back at the castle, would they be able to get to Lorius? If they could deal with him, would there be a way of defeating the Umbrians, too?

And what lay ahead for him ... for him and his two friends? As Edwin stared at the canvas ceiling, he twisted the amulet round and round in his fingers, and wondered if Perpetua or Bellwin deserved to wear it more than he did.

They knew they were approaching the castle when the carriage wheels shuddered over stone cobbles. It stopped, then they heard the castle gates grind back.

'I did not think I would return home like this,' Bellwin said bitterly as the carriage lurched forward.

They sat shivering as voices echoed around the stable yard. Eventually the canvas was ripped open, and General Aquilla climbed in. 'A pleasant journey? You will be delighted to hear your elders are waiting for you in the courtyard. We have a surprise for you all.'

A guard unshackled their feet and tied their hands behind their backs. The yard was in half-darkness and heaving with Umbrian soldiers. Primus, Ollwin and Mersium stood in the centre of the yard, their hands also bound. Mersium was stooped, barely able to keep upright, and Ollwin's head was bowed. Only Primus still looked ready for a fight.

Aquilla led Edwin and the others over. Edwin stood next to Primus, with a guard on the other side. Edwin shot Primus a cautious glance. How could he tell him about Lorius and not give the game away?

'Where's Lorius?' he whispered.

'Taken prisoner, with the king,' Primus replied quietly.

'Look ... Lorius, he's –' Edwin paused as the guard glanced at him.

Primus leant forward. 'What?'

'He's –'

'Silence!' the guard growled. 'Our General is about to speak.'

Aquilla had climbed onto a balcony. He raised his hands and the courtyard fell silent.

'This day marks a new Umbrian era – the beginning of a mighty empire,' he began. 'I must thank our armies, who have carried out the most ambitious coup in Umbria's long and noble history.' There was a smattering of applause. 'There are others to thank – particularly one who, at great personal danger, laid our plans inside this very castle.'

Edwin glanced at Primus ... he was in for a shock. 'Umbrians,' Aquilla cried, 'I give you our hero. Hysterians, I give you your traitor.'

'I bet he hasn't got the guts to look at us,' Edwin muttered.

'He probably has,' Perpetua grunted.

'If I do not tear them from him first' Bellwin hissed.

Aquilla stepped aside as a door flew open. A figure shrouded in a hooded cloak stepped onto the balcony. There was a long pause. Edwin held his breath as the hood fell back …

CHAPTER FIFTEEN

THERE WAS SILENCE. THEN THE night air filled with Umbrian cheers. Edwin looked at Ollwin. He was staring straight ahead, his face aghast. Confusion seemed to paralyse Primus. Only Mersium's head stayed down, shaking as he struggled to speak.

'I don't believe it! Hercula!' Perpetua whispered.

'How could she do this to them?' was all Edwin could mutter.

Perpetua scanned the courtyard. 'Where's Malita? I bet she's in on this?'

Hercula raised her hands for silence. She bowed to Aquilla then turned to the crowd.

'My Hysterian friends –'

'WHAT FRIEND ARE YOU?' Primus yelled, his voice almost breaking. He barged forwards, but four Umbrian guards brought him down and they stuffed a gag into his mouth before dragging him away.

Edwin felt his jaw shake. 'Where is the king?' he bawled.

'Your father, Your Royal Highness?' Hercula said lightly. 'He is no longer monarch here – and no more royal than you!'

Laughter echoed around the courtyard, and Hercula descended the steps. She walked languidly towards Edwin, shaking Umbrian hands along the way. As she came close, Edwin thought her skin almost glowed white in the darkness. 'You did your best, Edwin,' she said softly. 'But we knew who you were all along.'

Edwin felt anger bubbling inside him. How dare she betray Janus. How dare she break Primus's heart. How dare she –

'Nothing to say?' Hercula continued. 'You are not so brave without Primus by your side.' She jabbed Edwin's chest. 'Or will the amulet protect you? I have decided you may keep it a little longer ... just for my amusement.'

Edwin's throat clamped. He glanced down.

'It is not, as I told you, a charm that protects its wearer from harm. Instead it draws the wearer to Umbria, and tells us how far the victim is from our soil.'

Edwin moaned and tried to wrench his hands apart. An Umbrian charm – he had to get if off ...

'How did this happen?' Ollwin snapped. 'Why did you wear it?'

Edwin stopped struggling. 'Because I trusted her. I'm so ... sorry ...'

'Sorry?' Hercula jeered. 'You are too late!' She swung around. 'Guards – take them away!'

Edwin, Perpetua and Bellwin were dragged to a side door. They entered a familiar passage, and Edwin remembered the first time he'd seen Janus's kind and gentle face. Now the king was going to die and Hysteria was going to fall to the Umbrians. Edwin felt a surge of nausea. Why had he listened to Hercula? Why had he trusted her? He hardly knew her ...

He was bundled down a flight of steps with Perpetua and Bellwin close behind, and they were thrown into the first empty cell the Umbrian guard could find. Perpetua winced with pain as she tumbled in. Edwin waited until the gate had been locked, then turned to Bellwin.

'Can you get this chain off me?'

'I cannot separate my hands.'

'Why don't you use magic? That's what you're trained for!'

'Have you forgotten?' Bellwin cried. 'Only Full Wizards can perform magic at free will – now I will never be one! Why did you accept that amulet ... this is your fault!'

'I know,' Edwin moaned. 'I'm so sorry, I -'

'Both of you – shut up!' Perpetua hissed, wriggling awkwardly to one side. 'Arguing will get us nowhere. Look!' She nudged her cloak. 'I've still got my dagger – it almost stabbed me when that horrible guard threw us in here!'

Edwin and Bellwin looked at each other and exchanged weak smiles. Edwin crawled to Perpetua, turned around and managed to clasp the hilt of the dagger behind his back.

'Can you slide the knife out?' Perpetua said. 'That's it ... up a bit ...'

The dagger slipped out. Edwin crawled over to Bellwin. 'Put your wrists straight out,' Edwin instructed, straining to look backwards. He felt the blade catch the rope and began to move it up and down. Perpetua edged over to supervise.

'Nearly there,' she whispered after a few minutes.

'My arms are killing me,' Edwin moaned, and just as he thought they were going to fail him, Bellwin's bounds snapped. 'Blimey!' Edwin gasped, slumping over his knees.

Bellwin rubbed his wrists. Thank you, Edwin. I am sorry for what I said – you were not to know Hercula was against us ... none of us did.'

'Doesn't matter,' Edwin said breathlessly. 'Just get this thing off me.'

Bellwin fumbled beneath Edwin's collar for the chain, then pulled it over his head.

Bellwin peered at the amulet. 'What is that writing?'

'Dunno,' Edwin replied. 'Hercula said it was some old language.'

Bellwin steadied the amulet with his fingers. 'It is probably Umbria's second tongue – there are a few words familiar to me.'

Perpetua frowned. 'How come?'

'Hysteria also has a second language – there are common words between ours and that of the Umbrians.'

'So can you read what it says?'

'Only these two words ... and the very first one – the name of Hereticus himself.' Bellwin raised his eyebrows. 'That means this charm could be his ...'

'Ugh!' Edwin groaned. 'And I've worn it ... that must be why I've felt a bit minging.'

'He means he felt unpleasant,' Perpetua said. 'I thought you were acting strangely, Edwin.'

'It is no wonder,' Bellwin added. 'The amulet is filled with the most vile Shadow

Magic – it would poison the mind and body of anything it touched.'

Edwin shook his head. 'That explains why the petris flowers died. Why didn't I realize?'

'Well, it's no good worrying now,' Perpetua said tartly. 'What's done is done. Bellwin, these other words you recognize – what are they?'

'They say bloodless creatures.'

Perpetua pulled a face. 'That's interesting. Can someone free my hands, please?'

Edwin watched Bellwin sever the ropes around Perpetua's wrists. He closed his eyes and tried to think. Something was coming together. Edwin felt Bellwin start on his hands. Suddenly he shot to his feet.

'I know what this means!' Edwin shook off his ropes.

Perpetua and Bellwin sat back, wide eyed.

'The Umbrians are vampires!' Edwin cried. 'Shadow Magic changes the physiology of those who use it, right – bloodless creatures could be the vampires themselves, or the creatures they feed on.' He scraped his hands through his hair. 'It all fits with how the amulet made me feel. I hated bright light ... I kept having dreams about the dark. And when Primus killed the giant I couldn't stop staring at its blood.'

Perpetua sat up. 'And it makes some more sense of the name Shadow Magic – vampires don't cast shadows ... what could make a shadow conspicuous? When it doesn't exist!' Her face fell. 'One thing, Edwin – at home, vampires in books and films can't go out in daylight ... and we've seen Hercula around in the daytime.'

'But don't you remember – Eifus told me that lots of species evolved differently here ... and the sun isn't very strong.'

Perpetua nodded. 'Hercula looks really pale ... maybe she keeps out of direct sunlight, like you wanted to.'

'She's the one we've got to get first,' Edwin said. 'We have to kill her!'

'But how do you kill a ... what did you call it – a vampire?' Bellwin asked. 'No one has ever learned how to kill an Umbrian wizard.'

'Everyone knows how to kill a vampire,' Edwin replied haughtily. 'You have to drive a stake through its heart!'

'And where are we going to get one of those?' said Perpetua. They scanned the cell, but drew a blank.

'There's the sunlight thing,' Perpetua added. 'But we know Hercula can withstand that. I'm sure there are other ways, Edwin.'

'Yeah, but I can't think what they are ...' Edwin's eyes suddenly lit up. 'Bellwin – have you still got that reading stone?'

Bellwin fumbled inside his cloak and held the stone up.

'My encyclopedia's in my room – can you do that spell so I can read it?'

Bellwin looked terrified. 'Now? I ... I have seen it performed only once.'

'Y-e-s,' Edwin said slowly. 'But Ollwin told you to look closely. You did look closely, didn't you?'

Bellwin glanced at Perpetua. 'Of course, but ...'

She jumped up. 'And so did I! We've got you through two spells, Bellwin – we can get you through a third!'

Bellwin reluctantly placed the reading stone in his palm.

'That's it,' Perpetua said. 'Now, blow on it twice.' Bellwin took a very deep breath, but blew barely enough air to flutter a daisy chain.

'No,' Perpetua said frostily. 'Harder – try again!' This time Bellwin blew so hard that his cheeks turned puce.

'That'll do,' Perpetua instructed. 'Now close your fingers. No, not like that – Ollwin said the pressure had to be just right.'

For a few seconds there was nothing then, suddenly, smoke began to trickle from between Bellwin's fingers.

'Fantastic!' cried Edwin. 'You did it!'

'I was supervising,' Perpetua added lightly. 'What's your encyclopedia called, then?'

'The Popular Book of Facts and Fables.'

'OK, Bellwin – you know what to do.'

Bellwin glanced from Perpetua to Edwin, looked at his hand, then muttered, 'Edwin Spencer's Popular Book of Facts and Fables.'

The trickles of smoke quickly turned to cloudy plumes. They swirled and gathered into a circle, and once again the centre cleared into a glassy panel. The first pages of a book came into focus: it was Edwin's encyclopedia, with Aardvark as its top-most entry.

'I have done it!' Bellwin gasped as he gazed into the circle. 'Find the letter V.'

The book's pages flipped over and back again between B and D.

'It hasn't got any better at the alphabet,' Perpetua scoffed. 'Come on, go a bit further!'

The book slapped shut. There was a sulky pause, then it fell open at a large letter V. The corner of the page snapped down: There, it seemed to say.

Perpetua leant forward. 'Over ... over ... stop. Here we are!' she yelped. 'Vampires!'

Edwin blinked. '"Vampires – subject of Eastern European folklore, portrayed as surviving on the blood of living creatures. Fable tells they can be killed by exposure to sunlight, contact with purified water or puncture through the heart with a wooden stake".'

'Oh ...' They all sat back looking very deflated.

'We can't conjure up purified water,' Perpetua said. 'There's more chance of finding a stake.'

'But if vampires here are not hurt by sunlight,' Bellwin replied, 'how can you be sure that a wooden stake would work?'

Perpetua shrugged. 'It'd be worth a try – what's the alternative?' She creased her nose. 'Bellwin, are you all right?'

Bellwin's face had almost turned grey. His lips were blood red, his eyes were wide. 'I think ...'

'What?' Perpetua whispered. 'What's the matter?'

'It is incredible, perhaps Ollwin was trying to tell me ...'

'Tell you what? Spit it out!'

'My final apprentice task ... I think I have just completed it.'

CHAPTER SIXTEEN

'EH?' EDWIN SAID. 'How D'YOU KNOW? Ollwin hasn't given you a pass.'

'Do you not remember what I told you – the master is not needed for the final task,' Bellwin replied. 'The vortex itself senses the completion I can feel it is trying to convert me, but ... but something is not right …'

'OH ... MY ... GOODNESS!' Perpetua gasped. 'Then get us out of here! How can we find the others? Where will Janus be?'

Bellwin gazed at her. 'I have just realized –'

'Let's tackle their army first. D'you need some kind of wand?'

Bellwin raised his hands. 'Perpetua, you do not understand, the –'

'But I –'

'LISTEN TO ME!' Bellwin hissed. 'If things were as usual, I would now be a Full Wizard. But the vortex needs a great deal of power to convert an apprentice.'

Perpetua's face fell. 'Oh, no …'

Bellwin sighed, 'And there will not be enough.'

Edwin slumped back. A ray of hope had glinted in the distance, then snuffed itself out. 'So you still can't cast spells at free will?'

'Not in time to help us.'

Perpetua's face crumpled. 'But I want to go home! Just do it, Bellwin – just do it!'

'Perpetua!' Edwin snapped. 'Have you lost the plot completely? Bellwin can't perform magic at free will until he's a Full Wizard. It's like you going for the Nobel Prize for Physics when you haven't passed your GSCE!'

'I was going to take it next year,' Perpetua sniffed. 'Lorius said I was good enough …'

Edwin let it go. He could see Perpetua was a girl-on-the-edge.

At that moment three guards stomped down the passage. Keys rattled in the lock and the gate swung open. 'Out!' said a gruff voice.

Edwin got up first, crossing his hands behind his back, and Perpetua and Bellwin copied him Very soon Edwin realized they were heading for the throne room. He was dragged up the steps of the Great Hall and the archway opened up. This time an Umbrian stood guard, leering as they were bundled through.

What confronted Edwin made him gasp. The room was lined with Umbrian soldiers. Hercula sat on Janus's throne. Aquilla stood to one side and a guard stood to the other, his hands pressed around an ornate wooden spear. Behind them, the vortex's glow was still soft and muted. Ten metres away from Edwin five men were crouched on the floor, their hands bound. Lorius, Mersium, Primus, Ollwin and, in the centre, his face etched with pain, knelt King Janus.

Edwin tried to bolt towards him. 'JANUS!' he yelled as he was dragged back. 'No! Don't touch him ...'

Perpetua gave a muffled sob. 'Edwin, there's nothing we can do!'

Aquilla waited for silence, then raised his hands. 'We are all here – at last our entertainment may begin! We have King Janus and the most favoured of his court, lined up like slaves in a market auction.'

Edwin looked at Primus, but the knight's eyes were fixed on Hercula. Come on, snap out of it, Edwin thought. You're the hero ... get up and fight!

Aquilla descended the steps from the throne and walked behind Lorius. Aquilla produced a knife and put it to the nape of Lorius's neck. Edwin's chest froze and he felt Perpetua push her face to his shoulder. Aquilla slashed the blade down Lorius's tunic, then ripped the cloth apart. Edwin's legs started to shake. He knew exactly the preparations Aquilla was making.

Aquilla did the same to Mersium and Janus. He moved on to Primus, but let his blade catch Primus's neck so his tunic fell apart speckled with blood. Primus didn't flinch; he was still staring at Hercula, his expression shot through with bitterness.

Ollwin was last. Aquilla tore his tunic, then pushed him to the floor.

'No!' Bellwin whimpered. 'Master ...'

Aquilla turned to Hercula and bowed. She stood up, descended the steps and walked down the line of prisoners, looking at each one with disdain. Edwin swallowed. How would she treat the ordinary people of Hysteria? The farmers, the millers, the cooks, the teachers; the little girl who gave Edwin flowers – what was going to happen to her?

'You have finally relinquished Hysteria to the Umbrians,' Hercula said. 'It will be a pleasure to see you all die. You may take to your graves the knowledge that each and every Hysterian will be enslaved, and that Umbria will conquer every kingdom in these territories.'

Hercula walked back down the line. She suddenly paused at Mersium and reached out and it seemed for a moment that she might touch his face. But Hercula moved away. 'There has been no greater traitor to their family!' she snarled, climbing the steps. 'You will die first Mersium' Aquilla – begin!'

Aquilla gave a signal. 'Executioner!'

A giant of a man stepped from a line of soldiers and pulled a black visor over his face. He strode to the middle of the room, the curved blade of his axe glinting in the torchlight.

Edwin began to shiver. 'Oh, no ... please no ...'

Mersium was still barely conscious, but two guards hauled him to his knees, dragged him over the flagstones and propped his chest upon a large wooden block. Aquilla reached down to grasp tendrils of his hair. 'Ready yourself to die,' he cried, raising Mersium's head.

The executioner lifted his axe. Aquilla looked up, his mouth contorting with delight. Edwin held his breath and pulled Perpetua closer. He raised his gaze to the ceiling. He couldn't look at this he couldn't look ...

There was an agonizing pause.

Aquilla yelled, 'Now!'

BOOM!

The vortex exploded to life. White light crackled and towers of flame flashed to the ceiling. Aquilla screamed and leapt forward as the axe fell. The blade missed Mersium's neck but came scything down into Aquilla's leg. The axe rose and the executioner staggered back. Blood pumped from Aquilla's wound. He spun around, crying, baying for help, and slipped in the red liquid splashed across the floor.

Edwin felt Perpetua wrestle free and they gazed at the vortex, their faces lit orange.

'It's working,' Edwin murmured. 'It's actually working ... but how?'

'It does not matter,' Bellwin yelled. 'I ... I can feel it coming ...'

Bellwin clutched his throat and slumped to his knees. The vortex began to hum and he doubled up; the next second he was encased in light. An arc of silver crackled to Bellwin's temple then quickly melted away. He retched, sat up and wiped his lips. 'It is done,' he said breathlessly. 'I am a wizard!'

A scream brought everyone to their senses. Hercula staggered down the steps, staring wildly at Aquilla. Edwin dragged Bellwin to his feet then scanned the room. It swum before his eyes, his thoughts chasing each other in a frantic whirlwind. What to do now ... how to save Janus ... how to ...

Edwin fixed on the guard next to the throne and pointed straight at him. 'Bellwin – release the wooden spear ... break off the end!'

'Extricatium ligneous ... seperatum!'

The spear shot from the soldier's grasp and broke in mid air.

'Release Primus's hands.'

'Extricatium ligature!'

Primus stood up.

'Give him the wooden stake !'

The spear's end streaked towards Primus. He jumped to catch it.

'PRIMUS!' Edwin bawled. 'STAB HER THROUGH THE HEART!'

At that moment the Umbrian guard surged forward. Edwin looked at Bellwin, but he was one step ahead. 'Umbrian legionaria desensonarium!'

The soldiers fell to the floor, toppling together like rows of dominoes.

Primus moved towards Hercula, the baton's jagged point jutting from his fist. She edged away but he followed, stalking with slow, precise steps.

'No …' Hercula pleaded.

'No, my lady?' Primus snarled. 'But this is what you planned tonight – death!'

Primus leapt at Hercula like a ravenous lion. He grabbed her neck and raised the stake, then plunged it into her chest. Hercula threw back her head and screamed, then gasped in a breath and gazed at Primus, her mouth quivering.

Primus showed no mercy. He pushed Hercula to the floor, then strode over to Aquilla through the gathering pool of blood. He took Aquilla's sword and without hesitation ran it into Aquilla's stomach.

'He has almost no more blood to shed,' Primus murmured, drawing back the blade. Then he glanced up. 'Lorius, help me with Mersium.' Primus and Lorius lifted Mersium from the wooden block and carried him to Janus and Ollwin. Edwin and Perpetua ran to join them.

'Are you all right, Your Majesty?' Edwin whispered.

'Yes ...' Janus replied, looking at Mersium slumped before him. 'How could Hercula do this to us?'

Edwin grabbed Primus's arm. 'We think she's a vampire!'

'A vampire?' Ollwin said. 'What –'

'They're creatures that live on blood,' Perpetua cut in. 'And they ... oh, but that doesn't matter now – the wooden stake should've killed her!'

Then I must try and finish the task,' Primus growled, still gripping the hilt of Aquilla's sword. He looked across to Bellwin. 'Can you take the poison from Mersium's body?'

'I can use a spell to disperse it.'

'Do so, quickly – before he dies! How long will the Umbrian guard be unconscious?'

Bellwin's jaw hardened. 'For as long as I choose.'

Primus turned to Janus. 'Your Majesty,' he said gently. 'Stay here with Mersium No-one will harm you now – Lorius and Bellwin will look after you.' He suddenly looked around and said, 'Where is Hercula?'

Edwin's stomach lurched. Perpetua leapt up and they both scanned the room. 'She's not here,' Edwin murmured. Then his eyes fell on red circles that had splattered through a doorway. 'But ... but I can guess where she's gone.'

Everyone sat up and followed the line of his gaze.

'To the mausoleum ...'

CHAPTER SEVENTEEN

PRIMUS RAN ACROSS THE ROOM, followed by Edwin and Perpetua with Ollwin behind. They tracked the trail of blood along the passage and scrambled down damp stone stairs, the air growing colder with every step.

By the time they'd reached the mausoleum the red splashes had merged into a line. Primus raised Aquilla's sword and passed through the open doors. He stopped, beckoned the others to follow, and they gathered behind him. Their eyes adjusted to the semi-darkness. Hercula was draped over Auvlin's body and Malita cowered in the corner, hiding her face in her hands.

'Is Hercula dead?' Perpetua whispered.

'NO!' Hercula screamed. 'Death is slow for one of my kind!' She stood up and a river of blood pumped down her dress. Her legs gave way and she slid to the floor. 'Edwin,' she said, her head swaying. 'You have surpassed my expectations. I saw little of this initiative in your pathetic world.'

Edwin's mouth gaped. What was that?

'You've been to Earth – but how?' Then, it hit him, and Edwin said, 'That's how you knew what a lullaby was ...' But his blood froze. 'You went to Templeton Grove? You went to my home?'

Hercula shook her head. 'No – to your school.'

Edwin frowned, struggling to understand. How could she ... but suddenly he realized. The pale skin, the sunglasses, the strange feeling of familiarity when he'd first met Hercula.

'You were Miss Dawson,' Edwin said slowly. 'When Lorius first told me about Hysteria, you walked past the classroom – it was you who told Aquilla I'd cried.'

Hercula smirked. 'Yes – I followed Lorius to Earth, after Auvlin had been dealt with.

Edwin felt a swell of anger. Was it you that killed him ... or did you get someone else to do your dirty work?'

'Oh, no – the honour was all mine.'

'But how?' Ollwin said quickly. 'Only Mersium could hold his dagger – it recognized his body chemistry alone.'

Hercula stared long and hard into all their faces before she replied, 'Because I am not Hercula of Oreon. I was transformed into her image, but she lies rotting with the rest of her miserable family. No, I am Mersium's twin – Mercia.' She gave a hollow laugh. 'Did he not tell you all about his family? And we were so close …'

Ollwin clutched his chest. 'You are his twin?'

Mercia gave a triumphant nod. 'It enabled me to hold his dagger. Only for a few seconds – but it was enough to strike one glorious blow.'

There was nothing to be heard but shocked silence. Edwin's gaze was met by one bewildered stare after another.

Primus was the first to speak. 'Mersium was trying to tell us when we found him.'

'Yeah,' Edwin added, 'and we thought he was begging for mercy.'

Mercia took a convulsive breath and said, 'He was a traitor to the last.' She looked at Malita, who was still cowering in the corner. 'I am dying, Malita – my magic will die with me. You cannot sustain the charm over the body once I am gone. But we were almost –'

Ollwin sprang forward. 'Auvlin's body?' he growled. 'What magic have you cast?'

Mercia strained a smile. 'The grand coup – we had almost merged the soul of Hereticus into the body of your prince.' She closed her eyes for a moment. 'Our mighty leader is dead, but I took his soul with Shadow Magic and kept it ... kept it in hope we would lay a plan – one that would bring him back and destroy Hysteria's monarchy.'

'That ... that's horrible,' Edwin whispered.

'Thank goodness,' Ollwin said. 'Thank goodness we stopped the spell in time.'

'But we almost succeeded!' Mercia spat. 'How glad I would have been to give Janus the news – who knows, we may not have needed the axe ...'

'In the name of Hysteria!'

Primus lunged forward, knocking Ollwin aside. He gripped Mercia's shoulder and rammed the wooden stake deeper into her chest. Mercia fell back. Her lips quivered, her eyes fluttered to a close, a gurgling moan escaped her throat and her chest froze still.

'Is she dead now?' Perpetua whispered.

Everyone held their breath. Primus stood up and kicked Mercia's lifeless hand onto her stomach. 'Yes,' he snarled, and flung Aquilla's sword across the room.

Dozens of footsteps echoed outside, and a dozen Hysterian soldiers rushed in.

'Take this body away,' Primus told them. 'And put this servant into the darkest, most rat-infested dungeon you can find.'

A white-faced soldier stepped forward. 'And the Umbrian guard, my lord? They are asleep all over the castle.'

'They will remain so until Wizard Bellwin releases them.' Primus wiped his hands, smearing trails of blood down his tunic. 'Ollwin, the spell that Mercia spoke of – what does it mean?'

But Ollwin was already standing by Auvlin's body. He placed fingers under the wrist, and within a moment his breath quickened. He looked up, tears welling in his eyes, and whispered, 'He is alive.'

CHAPTER EIGHTEEN

EDWIN KEPT LOOKING BACK AS they walked towards the throne room. He still couldn't believe what he'd seen: this boy, this body, had woken, sat up and asked Edwin who he was. It had certainly taken a lot of explaining. Edwin hadn't been able to say anything at first but Perpetua soon found her voice. She'd introduced herself, told the story from their side, and had even helped Auvlin down from the marble plinth.

'His hands are quite warm,' she'd said to Edwin. 'You'd never known he's been dead for all this time.'

And now Edwin was leading them back to the Throne Room, with Bellwin and Primus propping the prince up.

'I can't wait to see Janus's face!' Perpetua said. 'I hope it's not too much of a shock.'

But what met them in the Throne Room was very unexpected. Janus was back on his throne and Mersium sat at his feet. His hair was dishevelled, his face was dirty, but his eyes were bright and alert. He sprang up when he saw Edwin.

'Janus has told me everything,' Mersium said as they shook hands. 'I cannot find the words to thank you.'

Edwin felt a bit awkward. He'd almost convinced himself that Mersium was Hysteria's traitor. Should he confess, before someone else let it slip?

'Don't worry about it,' Edwin mumbled. 'It was, er …'

'But you don't understand!' Mersium said eagerly. 'Not only have you saved all our lives – including that of my dear friend Janus – you have saved Hysteria from Umbrian rule. Slaughter ... slavery ... Shadow Magic – there could be no worse a fate.'

Edwin gazed at Mersium. His portrait hadn't done him justice – yes he looked strong and brave, but it hadn't caught the real warmth of his eyes. If only Edwin could have known from the start.

Janus got to his feet and walked towards Edwin, his expression haggard and strained. But halfway over he stopped. Edwin stood to one side, then Perpetua, and the king caught his breath.

Ollwin and Primus helped Auvlin take shaky steps. Auvlin looked up. The king hesitated, his lips began to tremble. He raised his hands and reached out. A shrill cry escaped him, and Auvlin fell into his arms.

'Father ...'

They knelt to the ground and Janus buried his face in the prince's hair. 'My son ...'

'Should we leave them alone?' Edwin mumbled, his heart almost bursting. This should be behind closed doors.'

Perpetua sniffed. 'That means –'

'Perpetua,' Edwin sighed, fighting the lump in his throat. 'They know ...'

It was the middle of the night but no one could sleep. Janus and Auvlin had spent a few hours together, then everyone had been summoned to the dining hall. Edwin and Perpetua got there to find a huge fire blazing and a table set with nine places. Primus, Mersium and Lorius arrived next, then Ollwin and Bellwin Last, walking into the hall arm in arm, came Janus and Auvlin.

Ollwin stepped forward to help Janus, but was waved away. 'I have my son to help me now,' the king said. It wasn't until the meal of bread and meat had been served and the goblets filled with wine, that the conversation truly began.

'I am tired, but there is so much to discuss,' Janus said. He patted Auvlin's hand. 'My recovery will start tomorrow – it will be quick, now I have my heir by my side.'

Edwin half-smiled. He was glad to see Janus so happy. The king had got back the thing he wanted most. Then shame washed over Edwin. He felt jealous - Auvlin had what Edwin wanted most. But he put on a brave face. 'How d'you feel?' he asked Auvlin.

Before the prince could reply, Perpetua chimed, 'It's amazing! You were dead for –'

Ollwin raised his hand. 'That is not strictly true.'

'But his body was cold – Lorius said so!' Perpetua looked back at Auvlin. 'At home we'd probably call you a zombie. That's a –'

'Yeah, whatever!' Edwin snapped. He shot Perpetua a look. Her tact-o-meter was definitely on the blink.

'Auvlin's body was in a state of suspense,' Ollwin continued. 'He did die, but he was brought back to life very quickly, with the soul of Hereticus planted within.'

'So how was it done?' Bellwin asked.

'Hercula must have cast the spell as Auvlin lay dying – the magic awoke the moment he gave his last breath, protecting the last tiny flicker of life.' Ollwin thought for a moment. 'I was surprised how well the preservation spell worked. I should have trusted my instincts.'

'So what would've happened if Mercia's spell had run its course?' Perpetua asked.

'Auvlin's corpse would have come fully alive, with Hereticus as its master.'

'Blimey,' Edwin croaked. He looked at Auvlin. 'And you feel all right after that?'

'I am weak, but well,' Auvlin replied, then he smiled. 'I cannot get used to the sight of you, Edwin – it is almost like having a brother.'

'And you would be proud to call him so,' Janus said. 'Edwin has saved Hysteria, there is no doubt.'

Edwin looked down and swallowed hard. 'I don't know about that,' he mumbled. 'What about Bellwin – we couldn't have done it without him.'

'And I could not have reached Full Wizarding without you and Perpetual Bellwin said firmly. 'But something puzzles me, how did the vortex suddenly reach full power?'

Lorius coughed. 'That is my doing.'

All eyes turned to him.

'You?' Ollwin whispered. 'But only full wizards may work with the crystals.'

Lorius glanced up nervously. 'I have been ... experimenting, in the privacy of my rooms. I know I am not permitted to work with magic, but –'

'How long have you been doing this?' Ollwin demanded.

Lorius threaded his fingers. 'For over thirty years.'

'WHAT! Since you gave up your apprenticeship? But you chose science over magic!'

'I wanted to practise both,' Lorius said. 'Magic still drew me ... I could not resist.'

'So what did you do,' Ollwin grunted, 'to make the vortex spring to life?'

'It took many years to perfect the formula,' Lorius replied eagerly. Edwin had never seen him look so enthusiastic about anything. 'An amalgam containing three crystals is placed inside the vortex. Auras build, and power is concentrated until the amalgam bursts. I put one in the vortex before you left for Umbria – what we saw tonight was the result.'

Ollwin drummed his fingers. 'A timely experiment,' he conceded. 'I suppose I must forgive your transgression, for without it we would all be dead.'

'So that's what you were doing in your room,' Perpetua said. 'We did wonder.'

Lorius met Perpetua's gaze. 'I know,' he said slowly. 'I am aware you had your suspicions of me.'

'For good reason!' Edwin blurted. 'Why did you take Mersium's dagger ... and why did you hide it in secret?'

Janus raised his hand. 'Lorius's conduct was entirely honourable.'

'So you know about it?'

'Lorius told me a few hours ago. He was sure Mersium had not attacked Auvlin, but he wanted proof. He took the dagger from my son's body and his hand was burned by its hilt – he knew this could have some significance, so he kept the dagger for experimentation. He told us his scar had come from a riding accident.'

Lorius fixed on Edwin. 'I have a question for you –what were you all doing outside the mausoleum that day?'

'We were trying to find the court record. Bellwin conjured an orb and when you

338

found us it'd just slipped through the door.'

Ollwin sat forward. 'I think it was Malita who hid the record – to prevent your investigations. And we now know she had access to the mausoleum key.'

'But how?' Edwin asked. The king had it on a chain.'

'I was also the subject of Shadow Magic,' Janus replied. 'It first compelled me to have Auvlin's body preserved, then it altered my pattern of rest – occasionally I fell into a heavy sleep, and Malita would take the key and visit the mausoleum to nurture Mercia's spell.' He paused. 'It was a long process – once Mercia had cast the charm she could not risk being found in the mausoleum herself.'

Mersium turned to Janus and grasped his arm. 'What can I say, my friend? My family almost destroyed Hysteria! My defection brought danger to this kingdom twenty years ago ... I should have guarded against it.'

'No, Mersium,' Janus said firmly. 'The blame does not lie with you, it lies with the people of Hereticus.'

'Hereticus!' Perpetua squeaked. 'What's happened to his soul?'

'When Mercia died her spell was incomplete,' Ollwin replied, 'so his soul would have passed from Auvlin's body. But his presence is no longer here – of that we can be sure.'

Edwin looked slowly around the table. Only a few hours ago things had looked as bleak as bleak could be. Now Hysteria was secure. Janus and his heir were alive and well. Who would've imagined it?

Primus studied Edwin. 'How long will you stay with us?' he said softly.

'I was just thinking, maybe we should go back home ... while everything's OK.'

'Before we ask you to help us again?' Janus said with a smile. 'But let us be serious – Hysteria owes you a great debt, Edwin, and we would like to thank you in some way.'

Edwin couldn't hide his surprise. 'Oh ... but you don't –'

'But we do,' Janus insisted. 'Our vortex is restored, but it will use a great deal of magic to send you and Perpetua home. We also have many dark auras to banish from the castle, but we can grant you one wish.'

Edwin couldn't quite believe it. What an opportunity! Maybe he could do better at school? He liked English, and he could impress his new teacher from the very start. But no, he should take his time. There might be something else he could use the wish for.

'Thanks, Your Majesty. Can I think about it?'

'Yes – you may tell Ollwin what you decide. So, do you want to return home tomorrow?'

Edwin looked at Perpetua, and she nodded. 'Yeah ... please.'

'As you wish. Now, it is late but we should take a little food ... and a little wine. Will you join me this time, Edwin? Junoberry cordial is not fitting for my toast.'

Edwin picked up his goblet and nudged Perpetua.

Janus thrust his hand in the air. 'To Hysteria,' he cried, 'and Edwin Spencer!'

CHAPTER NINETEEN

EDWIN AND PERPETUA SLEPT THROUGH their last morning in Hysteria. Edwin woke up at gone midday and wandered to Perpetua's room. She was reading a library book. 'I've never left one unfinished,' she said. 'And I don't intend to start now!'

They joined Janus and Auvlin for lunch, then Ollwin took Edwin to the spirit dungeon. Edwin had almost forgotten he'd have to go back to being twelve years old, and when he looked at his sleeves hanging over his hands, he felt a little bit sorry. But he cheered up when he told Ollwin how he wanted to use his wish.

They went back to their rooms to get changed. Edwin put his uniform on, but didn't look in the minor. He didn't want to see himself. He didn't want to see Edwin Spencer from Templeton Grove.

Perpetua burst into the room, bright and breezy. 'Are you ready?'

Edwin didn't reply.

'What's the matter?'

'I bet ... I bet I look a bit young now,' Edwin said finally. He touched his throat; he'd got used to his voice as it was.

'Yes,' Perpetua said pertly. 'Of course you do. But it's still the same old you, isn't it?'

Perpetua couldn't have thought of a worse thing to say. Edwin almost burst into tears.

'That's what I'm worried about,' he whispered.

Perpetua folded her arms. 'Edwin, have you forgotten everything you've done here?'

'Oh, yeah – a fat lot I did on my own! Leading the expedition to save Mersium . Primus was in charge. Fighting the guard in the Cave of Spells ... Primus killed it. Breaking into the fort ... Primus was ...' Edwin shook his head. 'The only thing that made me go on the rescue mission was the amulet – I thought I'd be safe.'

'None of that was your mission,' Perpetua said sharply. 'D'you know when your battle really started?'

Edwin looked up. 'No ...?'

'When you knew the amulet wouldn't save you. Who thought of asking Bellwin to read the encyclopedia – you. Who thought of breaking that wooden spear – you. Who was the first at Primus's shoulder when he followed that dreadful woman ...' Perpetua paused, and Edwin saw her bottom lip quiver. 'That was your courage ... it came from your heart. And no matter how old you are, or how tall you are, that heart still beats inside you.'

Edwin couldn't say a word.

Perpetua took a piece of paper from her pocket and opened it. On it were written VOLTAGE and EDWIN SPENCER in large round letters. Below were scribbled NERD ... SPEW ... CREEP.

'Remember this? I kept it the day you went home sick.'

Edwin blushed 'I was trying to take my mind off the voices ... I was only –'

'Is that what you thought of yourself?' Perpetua said softly. 'Is that how you thought others saw you?'

Edwin hesitated. 'Dunno.'

Perpetua took a pen from her pocket and thrust it into Edwin's hand. 'Don't you think you ought to try again?'

Edwin shrugged. 'Erm ... well ... there's nice,' he said limply. 'Or …'

Perpetua huffed and took the pen and paper back. 'You're missing the rather obvious ones,' she sighed, and wrote down two words.

Edwin looked at the paper, and blinked as he read

ED WINS

Edwin and Perpetua were silent as they walked to the Throne Room. Edwin's rucksack bounced off his hip, and his boots felt heavy after the delicate Hysterian shoes. As they passed through the archway Edwin wasn't quite sure what to expect. He didn't want some big, swanky send-off. But what he saw drew a sigh of relief. Janus sat on his throne with Auvlin and Mersium either side. Lorius, Ollwin and Bellwin stood at the foot of the steps. Primus was pacing the floor, seemingly lost in thought. Behind them stood Eifus and Dreifus, hopping from one foot to the other.

'Young master!' Dreifus cried. 'We greeted you on your first day in Hysteria, and now we are honoured to see you depart. What a story to tell our grandchildren!'

Eifus coughed. 'You forget, dear brother, you do not yet have any children. I fear you are too optimistic.'

'And what of it?' Dreifus retorted. 'Of late many young ladies have looked upon me with favour.'

'Really?' Eifus said, perking up. 'And have you told them you have a twin?'

Dreifus smiled. 'Of course, brother dear – identical!'

Perpetua giggled. 'Do we really have to go now? We could stay just a little bit -'

'It's the right time,' Edwin said firmly. 'Richard Sweet could be setting fire to your science notes right now!'

Perpetua smiled. 'Come on then ... let's get this over with.'

Edwin turned to Ollwin first. The wizard grasped Edwin's hand. 'What can I say, my friend? What expectations we had ... how much you have exceeded them all.'

Primus strode to Edwin and clutched his shoulder. 'It was an honour to fight with you – and I would gladly do it again. Good luck.'

Bellwin stepped forward. 'I hope we meet again, Edwin,' he whispered, then he flung his arms around him. 'Thank you ... I would not have reached Full Wizarding without your help.'

When it came to Lorius, Edwin offered his hand. 'No hard feelings?' he said.

Lorius hesitated. 'No,' he murmured, before shaking with the lightest of touches.

Edwin's legs began to shake as he walked up the steps to the throne. Mersium shook his hand, and then Auvlin, and it was only when he turned to Janus that his tears gathered.

'Goodbye, Your Majesty,' he croaked.

Janus stood up and gripped Edwin's shoulders, affection shining in his eyes.

'Goodbye, my son,' he said. 'I call you my son for that is how I regard you,

Edwin. You came here and saved my throne and my kingdom. No man could ask more of his heir.'

Edwin felt his chin wobble, and tears spilled onto his cheeks. 'I'm just Edwin Spencer,' he whispered. 'I'm just an ordinary boy.'

Janus pulled Edwin into his arms. 'Perhaps ... but one with extraordinary loyalty and courage.'

Edwin was enveloped in warmth. He felt Janus tremble He held on tight; so tight he might break him in two ... then Ollwin's hand was on his shoulder.

'Do not delay,' he said softly. 'Your Earth awaits.'

Edwin stepped back and wiped his nose on his sleeve.

He looked down as Perpetua climbed up the steps.

'Ready?' he said. 'It might be a bumpy ride.'

Perpetua gave a watery sniff and said, 'I won't worry if you won't.'

Edwin looked at Ollwin. 'Now?'

Ollwin nodded. 'Walk into the vortex and think of the time to which you wish to return.' He put his mouth to Edwin's ear. 'Remember – when you want to empower your wish, just say the words we rehearsed. The vortex will do the rest.'

Edwin fumbled for Perpetua's hand and she squeezed his fingers. He took one last look at Janus, then they walked towards the warm orange glow.

'When are we going back to?' Perpetua whispered as the heat hit their faces.

'Just before you followed me into that cupboard.'

'So I can get my science notes?'

'Er ... something like that.'

Air jolted out of Edwin's chest, and he found himself in the school playground.

'Why don't you just shove off?' a familiar voice said. 'I wouldn't play in your crummy five-a-side if you paid me.'

Edwin blinked and focused on Richard Sweet.

'Shut your mouth ... my dad says we're good.'

'Oh, yeah? My dad's seen you play, and he's seen your dad play as well, and he reckons you're both rubbish!' Edwin held his breath as Sweet and his gang piled in.

'Ed – help!'

This time Edwin didn't hesitate and he sprinted towards the thrashing pile of bodies. He grunted as he pulled back an arm, then a leg. Sweet's back was facing him, short red hair glistening on the fat folds of his neck Sweet raised his right arm, his fist clenched in a tight ball. Edwin lunged forward, gripped Sweet's elbow with both hands and pulled.

Sweet looked around, but didn't budge. 'Bog off, Spencer! Go and try someone your own size.' He wrestled free and turned back. 'Right ... you're gonna get it!'

Edwin took a gasp of air, then bent down and grabbed Sweet around the chest. He closed his eyes and whispered, 'Ascends imotion intimida!'

For a split second nothing happened. Then, with a force that almost dropped Edwin to his knees, he picked Sweet up. A lightning surge flashed through his limbs, and the next moment Sweet was skimming across the playground by the seat of his trousers.

One by one, the gang stood up. They looked at Edwin, then each other, then ran in all directions, leaving Sweet crawling towards the bike sheds.

Nat stood up and wiped a streak of blood from his nose. 'Blimey, Ed. How did you do that?'

'Just something I picked up. You all right?'

'Yeah ... thanks to you, mate. My football career flashed before me ... I thought I was gonna miss the trials.'

Edwin allowed himself a smile Nah ... not a chance. Come on!' He picked up his bag. 'I've got something to tell you. That déjàvu thing yesterday – well, you'd better brace yourself ...'

EPILOGUE

**Templeton Grove Comprehensive School
Stinching Lane, London N34 4BO
Headteacher: Mr I. M. Smellings**

**Mr & Mrs B. Spencer
64 Grove Road
Templeton Grove
London N34 3TA**

**22 December
Dear Mr and Mrs Spencer
I apologize for interrupting the
Christmas holiday, but I have some
interesting news!**

**As you know, last week our recently
appointed Head of Science, Mr Lorius,
disappeared without trace from the
school premises. I am afraid the police
have so far drawn a blank on his
whereabouts, and we are unable to locate
any family or friends.**

Imagine my surprise, therefore, to receive a letter from Mr Lorius this morning. I have, naturally, placed the letter in the hands of the Metropolitan Police, but I am obliged to pass on the content of this letter, as it concerns one of your children. I quote:

"Dear Mr Smellings
I would like to report an error in a Winter term report. The Science entry for Year 8 pupil Edwin Spencer should read as follows:
Grade – A. Comment – Good work.
Yours
Mr H. Lorius"
With all good wishes for the festive season. I. M. Smellings

ABOUT THE AUTHOR

J. D. IRWIN (who also answers to Julie) started writing Edwin Spencer Mission Improbable in 2001 when pregnant with her daughter. She'd been writing grown-up fiction on and off for many years, but maternity leave gave her a chance to have a serious stab at something else. She soon discovered that writing stories for children was much more fun, and from then on didn't want to write anything else!

You can find out more about J. D. Irwin and other Catnip books by visiting www.catnippublishing.co.uk